SKIES

NIC STARR

Intended for an 18 + audience only. This book is intended for a mature, adult audience. It contains graphic language, explicit sexual content, and adult situations.

CONTENTS

To the wonderful authors who took part in the Collier's Creek series, thank you. It was an amazing experience to spend time with you in our Collier's Creek world.

BLURB

Coming to Collier's Creek is the best decision they'll ever make.

When Kit arrives in the small town of Collier's Creek, he's searching for a change of scenery and the solitude to help him overcome his writer's block. All he wants is to be left alone to finish his novel.

Felix was born in Collier's Creek, with no plans to return. But after a nasty breakup and losing his job, he grabs the opportunity to help a friend by managing his coffee shop. He's not going to let life get him down.

Felix is drawn to the mysterious older man who says he wants nothing from him than conversation. But the sizzling looks hint at a lot more. Now he needs to convince Kit to ignore the town gossip about their age gap and theories about Kit's past, and to give them a chance. If Felix has his way, they'll find the happy ending they've both been searching for.

Blue Skies is a romance between a grumpy author and a barista full of sunshine who never expected to find love in the small town of Collier's Creek.

CHAPTER ONE

Kit

I leave a billow of dust behind me as I slowly navigate the winding dirt road in my Jeep. There's a brief moment of regret as I steer around another pothole, but this is what I was looking for—solitude and the beauty of nature. It's just a shame it doesn't come with a paved road. On the bright side, at least the neighbors are few and far between. After weeks of idly searching online, I'd chosen this place on impulse. Collier's Creek. The name evoked images of babbling brooks and nature's tranquility. Just what I need.

I round a bend and follow the directions they emailed—through the gates, past the main house where I've been told the caretaker lives, continuing along the gravel road until I come up to three cabins set well apart. Mine's the last of the three. The cabin sits alone in a sea of dark green trees, its weathered logs moss-covered with age. It looks like something from a travel brochure. *Authentic mountain retreat for your rustic getaway.*

I park alongside the cabin and kill the engine. The sudden silence is startling. There's no engine noise to drown out my thoughts, no more music to distract. I climb from the Jeep and take a deep breath, relaxing for the first time in months. A bird calls in the distance. Nothing but trees and birds, and glimpses of bright blue sky. *Perfect.*

After sucking in another few lungfuls of the fresh country air, I grab my bags and haul them into the cabin that's been left unlocked and waiting for me.

The cabin has a rustic feel and spartan furnishings, just as the online ad described. There's a stone fireplace and I can imagine sitting on the couch in front of a roaring fire with my laptop. A desk is by the window overlooking the woods, the ideal place for writing as it's bathed in the early afternoon sun. I dump my laptop bag there and check out the rest of the space.

The kitchen is basic but looks functional and opens into the living area. On the dining table, I find a welcome note and a set of keys, although in a place like this I'm not sure I'll even have to lock the door. The bedroom is at the back of the cabin, along with an attached bathroom.

It doesn't take long to unpack. I haven't brought a lot with me because I don't plan on doing much apart from writing. I shove T-shirts, jeans, sweatpants, and warm sweaters into empty drawers, along with underwear. My coat is in the back of the car. I'll grab it later. I dump the bag with my personal items on the bathroom counter, then wander back to the living room.

With everything unpacked, I boot up the laptop and stare at the blank document. My fingers hover above the keys, but words elude me and I sigh in frustration. But what did I think? That I'd arrive in Collier's Creek and sit in the cabin I've rented for the foreseeable future, and the book would magically write itself. *Fuck!*

I pinch the bridge of my nose. I've come up here for the solitude, to forget the past and to lose myself in my craft. I sigh again, flex my fingers, and begin to type. It's not the words of the manuscript, it's a dump of everything that's gone wrong in my life. They—whomever the hell they are—say that any words are better than no words and I'm hoping this is the case.

Perhaps putting my feelings to paper will help me move past whatever it is that's holding me back from writing my novel.

The sun dips below the tree line, shadows lengthening across the room. I'm surprised so much time has passed, but I focus back on my outpouring of frustration. I *want* to be free of the grief that still haunts me. I want to forget the drama and be able to look forward to the future, but even now there's a tightness in my chest that won't loosen. When I next raise my head, I'm in a darkened room, faintly illuminated by the light of my laptop screen. I only stop when my stomach protests that it's been too long since breakfast. Too bad I don't have any food.

The shower calls. I quickly wash, throw on a T-shirt and boxers, and crawl into bed. The sheets are cold on my skin, so I curl into a ball and wait for sleep.

I MUST HAVE FALLEN asleep some time during the night because when I wake, a dull light filters through the curtains. I'm tempted to roll over and pull the covers over my head, but hunger draws me from the comfortable cocoon I've made. The floor is cool beneath my bare feet, and the water from the faucet colder still. I brace myself before splashing my face, and washing the grit from my eyes. I don't dwell on my image in the mirror as I know what I'll see there—dark circles and hair in need of a cut. There's a towel on the rail next to the sink. I blindly grab for it and pat my face dry, but not before cold droplets run down my neck. *Shit! That's one way to wake up.*

Venturing to the kitchen, I open the fridge. In vain it turns out, because the fridge is bare, not that I expected differently. However, I'm desperate for coffee, so living in hope, and spying the coffee maker on the counter, I check the cupboards next. Success! An unopened can of ground beans. I'd prefer an espresso, but beggars can't be choosers, so the old drip filter it is. A short while later, I stand on the front porch sipping the hot brew and properly take in my surroundings.

The country air is crisp and fresh, scented with pine. A deer emerges from the trees, stopping to glance around before turning back the way it came. It's the perfect idyllic scene and a refreshing change to be surrounded by nature, but a familiar ache rises in my chest. The memory of happier times, when Mark and I had gone on adventures like this together. Sharing the wonder of nature, enjoying the simple pleasures in life. *Mark should be here with me.* We'd planned to grow old together in a place like this; me writing books in the peace and solitude, him enjoying his photography.

How did everything go so wrong?

I sink onto the hard swing seat, grief at my loss of the life I'd envisaged constricting my throat. I'd thought the move to Collier's Creek would dull the pain, but out here in the quiet wilderness, it only seems sharper. I place the coffee mug at my feet and bury my face in my hands, tears stinging my eyes, wondering if the hurt will ever fade. After a long while, I take a steadying breath and stand. There's no option but to keep going. I need to do this for myself; I need to rebuild my life, even if that life is alone. With that in mind, I pick up my mug and down the cooled coffee in one gulp, then head inside to shower and ready myself for the day.

THE DRIVE INTO COLLIER'S Creek winds through gentle mountain foothills. The sun makes an appearance, dappling light and placing shadows on the road. The shadows blend with potholes, making the journey an adventure and making me thankful for my rugged Jeep. When I arrive in the town ten minutes later, it's everything I'd expected it to be—a bustling small town with quaint buildings and a charming rustic feel. I feel almost optimistic.

Parking in front of the general store, I make my way inside, grabbing a basket and filling it with essentials. At the register, a young woman with bright auburn hair and a friendly smile greets me.

"Morning. How ya doing?"

I know it's a standard question most likely asked by rote, but I'm taken aback for a moment. It's been a long time since someone asked how I am.

"Ah... I'm fine. Thanks."

"That's great. It's a gorgeous day, isn't it?" I'm flustered by the genuine warmth in her tone. I'm used to the anonymity of Seattle where they ring you up with speed and minimal conversation. For a moment, I regret coming into town and wish for the non-existent delivery service. She takes my basket and begins to scan the items. "You're new in town."

Is that a question or a statement? I nod. "Just arrived last night."

"You're up at the cabins, right?"

I blink in surprise. "How did you know?"

"Word travels fast in a small town like this." She laughs, eyes sparkling with amusement, then shrugs. "Actually, Shawn Mullins mentioned it. He's the caretaker at the cabins and said there'd be a new arrival staying for a while. I'm Georgia, by the way."

She holds out a hand, and I automatically shake it in return. "I'm Kit. Nice to meet you," I say, manners dictating my response, but in reality, the last thing I want is to be engaged in conversation.

"Hello, Kit. It's a pleasure." She focuses back on my groceries for a moment, ringing up a loaf of bread. "I've been trying to get Shawn to stock the cabins with a welcome pack of some basics, but it's been hard for him since his wife died.

I don't think he's quite got a handle on the stuff she used to do. If you need firewood, then Shawn's your man; milk and bread, not so much. Still, he's a good man. He'd give you the shirt off his back if you needed it."

I paste on a smile, but I have no idea what to say in reply. I haven't even met Shawn yet. All my interactions about the cabin booking were online, and I didn't even have to see anyone when I arrived. "That's good to know. Thanks."

She beams as she finishes ringing up my purchases. "Let me know if you need anything else."

"Directions to the nearest coffee would be great."

She seems thrilled to help. "There are a few places that do good coffee, but CC's is the best. It's just across the road. You'll meet Cam or Will this time of day. Cam's the owner."

"Right. Thanks." I nod at the unnecessary information overload. All I need to know is where to go for a decent espresso. I pay for my groceries and leave the store.

"See you next time," she calls out cheerfully before the door closes.

After placing my bags in the Jeep, I cross the road and enter the coffee shop. There's a gentle hum of conversation mingled with a country tune playing from somewhere out back and most of the tables are full. People sit by the window taking advantage of the sunshine. A cute blond guy sits by himself off to one side, tapping away on a laptop. It's cozy and inviting, but most importantly there's the aroma of fresh coffee.

I step up to the counter just as a guy holding a couple of plates comes out of the door to the kitchen.

He smiles. "Morning. I'll be with you in a moment."

After setting the plates down at a nearby table, he's back. "Sorry about that. I'm on my own this morning. Now, what can I get for you?"

"Just an espresso to go. Double shot. Thanks."

"Coming right up." He steps behind the machine and gets to work.

The sound of laughter draws my gaze to a table of women. They're of varying ages and I wonder what's brought them to the coffee shop today. Falling into old habits, my imagination goes into overdrive: fundraising meeting, church group, coven... My drink is ready before I can run through more than an idea or two.

"Did you want something to eat to go with that?" the guys asks as he passes over the paper cup. "I've got a fresh batch of muffins."

"Sure."

He places a berry muffin into a paper sack and I pay. As I leave, I meet the gaze of the guy with the laptop but quickly look away. I don't want to draw attention to myself. I want to spend my time in the solitude of the cabin and get this goddamned book finished.

During the drive back to the cabin, I drink my coffee and demolish the muffin, feeling better with some food in my stomach and a hit of caffeine.

Deciding there's no time like the present and *Peril in the Mountains* won't write itself, I make short work of unpacking the groceries and head over to the desk.

I've hardly typed more than a half dozen words when there's a knock at the door.

"Fucking hell," I mutter under my breath. "Can't a man be left in peace?"

I stomp across the room, pissed at the interruption, and wrench open the door to find a burly man standing there, toolbox in hand. "Morning," he says, grin so wide his white teeth stand out against his dark beard. "I'm Shawn. Thought I'd stop by and check you found the place okay."

"I'm here, aren't I?"

His smile fades, but he doesn't let my surly attitude stop him. "I'm the caretaker, so if you need somethin', just give me a holler. I live in the big house near the entrance. You can't miss it."

"I'm sure I'll be fine," I say, starting to pull the door shut.

"The hikin's mighty fine this time of year, fishin' too—"

"I've got work to do."

Shawn's brows draw together. "You should get outside, enjoy the scenery and fresh air. It'll do you good."

"I don't have time for that."

Shawn chuckles. "You'll change your mind."

Not likely, I think, not with the looming deadline. My phone rings. I incline my head toward the sound, grateful for the excuse to end this conversation. "Sorry, got to get that. Thanks for stopping by." I close the door on his puzzled face and hurry to the desk. My stomach drops at the sight of my agent's name on the caller ID, but I pick it up and answer. "Hey, Mike. What's up?"

"You didn't call. You promised an update on the manuscript."

I can hear his frustration. I grip the phone tightly as I glance at the open laptop. The document is mainly white space, the few lines at the top testament to how little I've gotten done over the past few weeks. My stomach churns at the thought of telling Mike. "Ah... it's coming along."

"I've got to say you have me worried, Kit."

"It's fine," I say, swallowing heavily.

"I'm not hearing much confidence in your voice, and there's a lot riding on this book."

I sigh. "To be honest, I've been in a rut, but I've moved out of town for a while. I'm hoping the change will spur things along."

"Where are you?"

"Just outside of a little town called Collier's Creek. Nature, mountain scenery, fresh air," I say, echoing some of Shawn's words from earlier as I pace the room.

"Well, I hope the change of scenery works. This is the last book in the series and expectations are high. Your fans want it written like yesterday and the publisher has a lot invested in marketing and promotion. In fact, about that—"

"Not now, Mike," I say, cutting him off. The quivering in my stomach increases. I can hardly get past chapter two of the damn thing, let alone think about book tours and media obligations. "I'll call you in a couple of weeks. We can talk then."

"Make sure you do." Mike's tone is short, but at least he's not pressing me. He can be a hard task-master, but he's been with me through the eleven books of the series so far and has become a friend.

"Thanks, Mike," I say with genuine gratitude, feeling like I can take a breath again. "I'll look at getting the first chapters to you next week."

As I end the call, I can only hope I'm able to deliver on my promise.

CHAPTER TWO

Felix

One day I'll learn to say no. But today isn't the day.

How can I turn Cameron down? I can't, not after everything he's been through. He deserves a break and to spend time with his new husband.

I sip my coffee, glancing around the coffee shop—it's got a real warm and welcoming vibe—before focusing back on Cam.

"And it's only for six months," Cameron says, winding up his sales pitch.

It's the same pitch he's already delivered over the phone. He either thinks I'm not sold on the proposition, or else he's feeling guilty about dumping it on me... Or there's another option. "Are you sure you aren't just trying to help me out?"

He barks a laugh. "Dude! Are you serious? You think I'd go to all the trouble of uprooting my life just to give you a job? I love you, man, but that's stretching the friendship."

"Hmm." I narrow my eyes and peer over the rim of my mug. "I'm sure there are better qualified people to run the coffee shop." I glance to the left where the espresso machine takes pride of place. "What about the guy behind the counter?"

He's older than we are, maybe in his mid-thirties, with a friendly smile, and I know he makes a mean cup of java because I'm sipping on one of his creations right now.

"Will? To be honest, I considered it, but he can't do the hours. He's a single dad and prefers working school hours. If you're worried you'll be stepping on his toes, don't be. He knows I've approached you."

"There's no one else?" I ask, because it's beyond me why he'd want me to be in charge of running things while he's away. I have experience in hospitality and administration, but it's his entire business he's trusting me with.

"Nope," Cameron replies. He throws a wolfish grin and waggles his brows. "You're it, I'm afraid."

"God help you and the poor folk of Collier's Creek, then."

His eyes light up. "So, you'll do it?"

"Pfft." I roll my eyes as I shake my head. "You think I drove across multiple states for a quick visit only to drive back home again right away?" *Home.* The word causes a funny feeling. I have no idea where that is anymore. They say home is where the heart is, but my heart's damaged and doesn't know where it belongs anymore.

"You'll manage the place for six months?" Cameron says, as if he needs reassurance.

I say the words he wants to hear. "Yes. I'll manage the place while you are gone." *It's not like I have anywhere else to be.*

Cameron thrusts his arms into the air and whoops. A cheer echoes from across the room. I glance to the counter and see Will giving a thumbs up. I guess he's happy with the news too.

"I can't thank you enough," Cameron says. "Greg will be relieved to hear it's all sorted. He didn't want me to put too much pressure on you, not after all the crap you've been through."

Immediately my defenses go up. "Oh, no! Don't you dare do that! I don't want a pity party—"

"It's not pity—" I narrow my eyes and throw a glare at Cameron. "Okay, okay," he says, "but we only want what's best for you. You deserve to be happy, Felix."

"I do," I say, projecting as much confidence in my voice as I can, because I *know* I deserve more than what's come my way lately. "Listen, Cam, I won't let it beat me. What happened may have left my heart a little bruised and battered, but I'll recover." *Damn, I hope that's true!*

"You never cease to amaze me."

I smile. "Yeah, well, enough about me. Tell me more about what's involved in running this place. Are you sure I'm up to it?" I say, changing the subject.

"Look around." Cameron indicates the coffee shop with a sweep of his hand. "We're not exactly doing a roaring trade. Usually there's just me and Will and a couple of part-timers who work during the busier times."

I've got to admit, now the lunch rush is over, things have quietened. The wooden tables that were previously occupied are now mostly empty, except one table with customers and the one where Cam and I sit near the window. An older lady is waiting for her order at the counter chatting with Will, who's tinkering with the coffee machine. A few people wander past outside.

"Are things going okay? With the coffee shop, I mean."

Cam shrugs. "I do okay. To be honest, CC's is never going to make a fortune, but it's never been about the money. Sure, I need to pay my bills, but it's more important to spend my days doing something I love."

"You love making coffee?"

"Hey, coffee is one of the world's greatest inventions." Cam chuckles, then grows serious. "I think you'll like it here too, Felix."

I wonder if he means CC's or the town. I choose to think it's the coffee shop he's talking about because I'm not too sure about being back in my hometown. I moved away reluctantly, but my family had grand hopes for me in LA; being back here feels like I'm returning with my tail between my legs. But I shove those thoughts away, focusing back on the present. I'm determined to make the most of the situation—I used to love Collier's Creek when I was a kid and I'm sure I'll be fine now I'm back.

"It's an amazing place, Cam. You've done an awesome job. This was the old general store last time I was here. Nothing like the new, bigger one across the street."

Cam chuckles. "You can't stop progress even in a small town like Collier's Creek."

I glance around the coffee shop. It's an older building that's been sympathetically restored. The exposed brick walls add a warmth that complements the wide polished floor boards that bear the signs of age. The counter also bears the patina of years of use, although the espresso machine looks futuristic. I like the furniture with its country cum industrial feel—wrought iron legs and reclaimed timber for the tabletops. Fresh flowers grace each table, and sunlight streams in the wall of windows at the front. The welcoming ambience is enhanced by the aroma of coffee, and the sound of country pop music softy piped through the room. It's very different to my old place of employment. There everything was bright and modern, the office filled with people and the noise of ringing phones and loud conversation.

Up until recently, I was an executive assistant to the retail buyer at a chain of menswear shops... My mood darkens at the thought of my ex-boss and Cameron must pick up on the change.

He leans forward and places a hand on mine. "I know you don't want to talk about it, but I'm here if you change your mind."

I nod. "Thanks."

Cam's my oldest friend, but that doesn't mean I'm dumping my shit on him. He's heard enough of my woes. Besides, I've made a pact with myself to get on with things—onward and upward, as they say.

"I mean it," he says.

"I know you do." I force a smile. "Now, tell me how this is all going to work."

Cam gives in and soon we're talking about rosters, and suppliers, and banking. The more I learn, the more confident I become. I may not have had responsibility for profit and loss before, and my only exposure to making coffee is my basic drip system, but I have enough business experience to feel confident I'll pick it up quickly.

"Plus, I'll only be a phone call away," Cam finishes. "Now let me introduce you properly to Will. You may remember him. He was on the high school football team, and you might have seen him play when you were a kid."

Will seems as friendly as his earlier grin suggested and welcomes me enthusiastically. We chat a little, and I get the feeling we'll get along like a house on fire. Thankfully, as it seems we'll be spending a lot of time together. Now my smile is genuine. Dare I say, I may even be a little excited at the prospect of what the next six months will bring.

AFTER PROMISING CAM I'LL join him and Greg for dinner, I say a quick farewell to Will. Stepping onto the sidewalk, I turn and look back at the building with fresh eyes—after all, it will be my responsibility soon. No more peeling paint and no more advertising posters plastered over the windows, instead fresh paint and shining glass. Two letter Cs and a coffee cup are emblazoned in one pane and potted trees sit on either side of the door. It's homey and welcoming.

I bark a laugh when I notice the old timber sign running partway along the length of the facade. It's the same sign that's been there for a long as I can remember—or most of the sign, at least. The part where it used to say *General Store* is completely missing. On the section that remains, the red lettering is faded away and only the letter C at the beginning of each word stands out. Those two Cs are the same font as those echoed on the window of the coffee shop. I love Cam's nod to the past in leaving the original sign. It's clear why the place is called CC's but I make a mental note to ask Cam more about it. Collier's Creek? Cam's Coffee? Coffee Capers?

I scan the street and memories come flooding back. It's a small town and I've been gone a few years, still I'm surprised that so much looks the same as it did last time I was here. The bookstore doesn't appear as if it's changed a bit. I wonder if old Mr. Ellis still owns the place. But as I look further around, I can see a few new stores, evidence of progress. People stroll along the sidewalk, a woman nodding as she passes.

Once upon a time, I couldn't walk around town without running into someone I knew. *Damn!* That thought jolts me from my reminiscing about the past and I hurry to my car. I'm not in the mood for a conversation about where I've been, and what I'm doing back, at least not yet.

I open the door of my Toyota. It's got over a hundred and fifty thousand miles on the dial, but it's still newer than the old rusted truck parked next to it. A car horn blows. Over the roof of the car I see a guy darting across the road, causing a car to brake. His coat collar is up at the back, but I catch a glimpse of his face as he turns and raises a hand in apology to the driver. Then his eyes briefly meet mine, a flash of unexpected bright blue. Something flutters in my belly, a frisson of something exciting. Before I can analyze it, he turns and ducks into the coffee shop. For a moment I regret I've left. I shake my head to rid the ridiculous thought and slip into the driver's seat. Obviously coming back to Collier's Creek is playing havoc with my emotions.

Maneuvering the car onto the road, I head to the place where I'll be staying for the next six months, but as I drive along the main street and head to the outskirts of town, it's hard to not continue my trip down memory lane.

CHAPTER THREE

Kit

The curser blinks on my laptop screen as words escape me. I stare at it a moment longer before giving up. I close the laptop with a sigh and rise from my desk, stretching to relieve the kinks in my back. You'd think I'd be used to spending hours working at my desk, but it seems to take less toll on my body when the words are flowing. However, right now every word is a struggle, despite all the hours I've forced myself to work on the manuscript. Obviously, the current approach isn't working.

After days of solitude, the cabin walls feel as if they're pressing in. As much as I hate to say it, maybe Shawn is right and getting outside in the fresh air will do me good. It's time I give myself a break from working non-stop. I vow to resume my morning jog. It probably wouldn't hurt to eat better too—I've been living on coffee, sandwiches, and canned soup—and that means a trip into town to stock up on fresh supplies.

An hour later, I'm parking across from the general store directly outside Ellis Books. I can't help myself—the lure of the bookstore is irresistible, so instead of crossing the road, I head to the store. I'm not disappointed when I enter, the familiar smell of paper and ink bringing a surge of happiness. A quick glance shows a cute blond guy serving someone at the counter, so I disappear down the aisle, walking between bookcases crammed full. My fingers trail the spines as I walk the aisle, slowing when I reach the mystery section. They have the latest bestsellers, and a wide collection of cozy mysteries too. My eyes land on *Mystery on the Mountain*, the first book in my *Mountain Mystery Files* series. I can still remember the thrill of seeing my book in print for the first time. I pick up the book and trace my name on the cover—Christopher Winters. My name on a book was a dream come true.

"It's a fabulous book. Have you read it?"

I nearly drop the paperback in surprise, gaze darting to find the man from the counter—the same guy I saw working on his laptop in the coffee shop last week—beside me. "Um. Yeah."

"The whole series is awesome. It's been really popular. Were you looking for one of the books? I'm still waiting on a back order of a couple, but we should have most of them in stock."

"No, thanks. I've read them all." I place the book back on the shelf.

"Oh. Then you must be hanging out for the next one. I hear it's the last book. I can't wait to see how it wraps up the series."

And there it is. My chest tightens at the reminder I have to write the perfect book bringing the series arc to a fulfilling close or else I'll be letting down thousands and thousands of expectant readers. I rub my sweaty palms on my jeans, as I murmur in agreement, then change the subject. "Do you sell stationery?"

"We sure do. Come this way and I'll show you what we've got. Are you after anything in particular?"

I shrug. "Just stocking up on some notebooks."

"Cool."

He leaves me to browse the selection. I grab half a dozen, snorting a wry laugh at my own wishful thinking—it'll take me months to fill the notebooks at the rate I'm going. I'm nearly at the register when an older lady gets there first with a book in hand.

"Good morning, Mrs. Hendricks," the guy says.

"Logan, dear. You look well." She places the book on the counter. "How's Cooper doing? I heard he's got a touch of the flu. Penny said he's recovering, but you can never be too sure with these kinds of things. Go back to work too early and you can have a relapse. Make sure you tell him to rest up. And I'm going to drop off some of my soup for you boys."

"That's awfully nice of you, Mrs. Hendricks, but totally unnecessary." The guy, who I now know is Logan, throws me an apologetic look, then reaches for her book. "Let me ring that up for you."

She keeps chatting as he completes her purchase and doesn't leave until he's promised to join her and someone called Gramps for supper one night soon.

"Sorry about that," he says as soon as she's left. "She has a heart of gold but loves a chat. Knows everything about everyone. It doesn't help that she's obviously been to the salon to have her hair done." He chuckles. "What is it about hairdressers? They love a good chat and Penny's no different."

I'm sensing that's a common theme in this town.

"No problem," I reply. "I'm not in a hurry." And I'm not, because what do I have waiting for me back at the cabin? Nothing but frustration. Procrastination is currently my friend.

Logan passes over the package of notebooks. "Well, thanks for your patience. Hopefully, we'll see you again soon."

Leaving the bookstore, I cross the road to the grocery store. I fall back on my usual habits and it doesn't take long to fill my cart and then history repeats itself as I find Mrs. Hendricks before me at the checkout. She's happily chatting with the girl I met last time, so I resign myself to another wait.

"I'm so happy that Logan and Cooper found each other." Mrs. Hendricks is in her element, eyes sparkling. "Isn't it wonderful? Our Cooper was alone way too long and Logan is such a dear boy. They're made for each other, and of course, it's perfect with Logan running the bookstore so that Gramps can retire. Cooper's leatherwork business is going well too."

I smile, thinking a romance between a bookstore owner and a leather guy could make an interesting story. My agent would hate it, of course, unless they ran around solving mysteries, but the idea appeals to me. Not that I need an agent to publish stories—self-publishing romance novels is the only thing that keeps me sane.

"You know," Mrs. Hendricks says, leaning in conspiratorially, "we have a betting pool on whether those two will finally tie the knot. I've got ten dollars on a Christmas wedding."

"Is that so?" Georgia says, putting the last of Mrs. Hendricks' purchases in a bag.

I'm taken with the idea. A Christmas wedding would be perfect for a story. My mind whirs with possibilities. It's almost disappointing when Mrs. Hendricks is on her way and it's my turn.

"Hey there, Kit," Georgia says, starting to scan my canned goods.

"Hello, Georgia."

She laughs, bright and loud. "You remembered my name. Well done."

I smile back. It's hard not to when faced with such an enthusiastic greeting.

A short while later I follow the same steps I'd taken on my first trip to town, and a few times since, dropping the bags to the Jeep and heading to the coffee shop. An espresso for the trip home seems a brilliant idea.

The aroma of fresh coffee greets me at CC's. It's busy with the lunch crowd, laughter and conversation buzzing. There's an empty table, but I head straight to the counter to place my order. I won't be staying.

The man standing there isn't the guy who served me last week. My heart misses a few beats as I take in the most gorgeous guy I've seen in recent memory. He has short wavy blond hair and warm brown eyes with the most disarming smile. Logan at the bookstore was cute, but this guy has my pulse fluttering and face heating. And when his dimple flashes, I go weak at the knees.

"Are you okay?" he asks.

It's then I realize he's asking me a question and has probably asked more than once. "Yeah, sorry. My mind was somewhere else." *God, I'm an idiot, standing here drooling over a guy who's* way *too young for me.*

"I was asking what I can get you, but from the looks of things, I'd say you're in desperate need of caffeine," he jokes.

I nod, finally regaining my senses. "And you'd be right. Espresso. Double shot. To go."

"Name for the order?"

"Kit."

"You got it, Kit," he says with another grin. He passes a cardboard cup to the guy working the espresso machine, then turns back to me. "Busy day?"

I shrug. "Just taking care of a few chores."

"Are you passing through town?" he asks with a friendly smile.

"Actually, I'm staying for a while."

His smile widens. "In that case, I'm Felix."

"Hi." I reach across the counter and hold out my hand, surprising myself by making the move.

Felix's hand is warm in mine, smaller and smooth. I don't want to let go. We lock eyes. His are brown, lighter around the pupil, framed with dark lashes. His smile is as warm as sunshine, lighting up his face. I tamp down the unwanted tug of attraction. I don't need complications.

The other man brings over my coffee, finally breaking the weird trance I'm in. I snap out of the hold Felix has on me and grab the cup. I barely remember to pay before putting my head down and hightailing it out of there.

On the drive back to the cabin, I make a resolution. No engaging in friendly banter with the charming barista, no getting distracted by those mesmerizing eyes and sunny smile. I am here to write, nothing else. I haven't been attracted to any man or a woman in recent times, so it should be easy.

Unfortunately, my brain doesn't get the message, and Felix lingers in my thoughts as I put away my groceries and get back to work.

An hour later, I'm still daydreaming about Felix and I know I'm not in the right headspace to focus on my manuscript. I close *Peril on the Mountain* with a hard tap of the keyboard.

The romance novel concept is playing in the corners of my mind.

I open a blank notebook.

A small-town romance with the Christmas wedding. It has all the makings of a Hallmark movie—sweet, sentimental, and guaranteed to tug at readers' heartstrings. My mood lifts at the idea of crafting the perfect romance—a story full of hope, and love, and happy endings. It's just what I need and I smile at the first spark of inspiration in days.

A romance between a bookstore owner and... what was he? Something about leather. Or maybe the other main character can work at the coffee shop next door, I muse. There's a strange flutter in my belly as I picture Felix with Logan. I scratch that idea without putting too much thought into why. Instead, I focus on my protagonists' motivation and conflicts. I jot ideas as I brainstorm, losing myself in the fictional world I'm creating. Soon I have pages of notes for a story where a broken-hearted man finds love in the most unexpected place.

I stare at my handwriting. What the hell am I doing?

I'm here to write my cozy mystery book, not rewrite my own love story. That chapter is closed.

Chapter Four

Felix

The sun filters through the window of the small kitchen, glinting off the glasses on the draining board, and dappling the faded linoleum floor. Everything looks tired and worn, and I make a mental note to have a chat with Uncle Shawn. He's been the caretaker of the cabins since Mom and Dad retired to Florida chasing the sun. He's been on his own since my aunt died, but now that I'm back, I resolve to see what I can do to help with the family business, at least in the short term.

I stand at the sink, rinsing out my coffee mug, when a flash of movement catches my eye. It's the guy from the coffee shop. *Kit.* He jogs past on the gravel road that winds its way through the property. Tanned arms pumping, sweat beading on his brow, his eyes flick up to meet mine for a brief second before he looks away again. My heart stutters at the flash of blue, the same way it did when I first laid eyes on him.

He continues down the road, leaving me staring at his back, my gaze glued to his broad shoulders and firm ass. I've never been more grateful for tight sweatpants that leave very little to the imagination.

It's only when he's disappeared around the bend it occurs to me he must be staying in one of the cabins. I wonder what's brought him to town. He doesn't seem like one of our usual vacationers here for hiking and fishing. Is he by himself or with family?

I chuckle to myself. It won't take long to find out on the Collier's Creek grapevine. Georgia most likely has all the info by now. If not, I can always hit up Mrs. Hendricks, although her facts aren't always reliable. Or I can check in with Uncle Shawn to see what information our guest provided on check in. *Fuck!* I'm as bad as them with my need for information, but I can't help it; he's piqued my curiosity, although probably not for the same reasons. I want to know more about the gorgeous stranger, but I'm not going to ask—he deserves his privacy.

A couple of hours later, I'm wiping down the counter at CC's when the bell on the door jangles. I glance up to see Kit stride in. He's wearing jeans and a dark sweater and I can't help picturing the fit body underneath the layers of fabric. His hair is swept back from his face, showcasing the perfectly groomed brows that frame his baby blue eyes that have me totally entranced.

He heads straight to the counter and my pulse speeds up at his approach, but before I can open my mouth, he speaks.

"Espresso. Double shot to go." His voice is gravelly, his tone, curt. I'm taken aback for a moment, but then he tacks on a belated, "Thanks."

"Sure thing."

Will's clearing some tables so it's up to me to make the coffee. It was challenging at first, but I've mastered the espresso machine, so I get to tamping the grounds. Once the machine is doing its magic, my focus turns to Kit. I catch him looking at me, but his gaze quickly focuses on the chalkboard menu. His fingers drum on the counter as he waits, but it doesn't take long and soon I'm back with the coffee.

"So you jog," I say as I pass over the cup.

"What?" His eyes flick to mine, brow furrowing.

"I saw you out for a run this morning. At the cabins."

"Oh, right." His frown deepens as he hands over cash for the coffee.

"There are some amazing trails up toward the mountains if you get bored with the route you took this morning." I give him the once over. "You look like you'd be able to handle something a bit more challenging."

He grunts in response, and I chide myself, feeling like a stalker. *Way to go, Felix.* I pass him his change, heat creeping into my cheeks.

"Thanks." Kit drops the coins into the tip jar, and pivots on his heel before leaving without a backward glance.

I stare after him, thoughtful, eyes glue to him until he passes by the front window.

I'm so zoned out that I jump when Will appears at my side. "So, what's the deal with tall, dark, and broody?"

"I don't know what you're talking about." I busy myself wiping down the already spotless counter.

Will nudges me with his elbow. "I saw the way you were watching him."

I toss the cloth into the sink. "I'm just curious about the new guy in town."

"Oh, is that what it is?" He leans in and whispers conspiratorially. "Don't worry, your secret's safe with me."

I lean against the counter and fold my arms. "There's no secret to keep."

Will shrugs. "If you say so."

"Will!"

"Okay, okay." He waves a hand, laughter in his voice. "Actually, there's not much to tell. He's been coming in for a couple of weeks but never stays to drink his coffee. He doesn't stop and talk to anyone, a bit of a loner."

"Interesting."

"Oh, yeah?" Will's grin turns sly. "Interesting how?"

I wave him off with a laugh. "We've got work to do."

I don't understand my fascination with Kit, a relative stranger, let alone have the ability to explain it to someone else.

He holds his hands up in surrender, laughing as he gets back to work.

PUSHING THROUGH THE DOORS of Jake's Tap, I'm assailed with memories. Friday nights spent hanging with friends listening to a band. Sunday afternoons watching the game or playing pool. Glancing around, it doesn't look as if much has changed. There's a game playing on the TV over the bar, regulars perched on the red vinyl barstools, and most of the tables are occupied. It smells of beer and fried food. Georgia waves me over from a booth at the back, the booth where we've spent countless hours chatting. She's the one person who gets me, and she always knows the right thing to say to help me gain perspective when I'm mulling over any of life's problems.

"There you are!" She grins broadly, a smile that I'm glad I get to see in person now. "I was beginning to think you'd stood me up."

"Never." I slide into the booth, snatching a fry from the basket in front of her.

"Hey!" she says in mock indignation, slapping my hand away. "Get your own."

I pout. "I'm hungry."

She pushes the basket toward me with a chuckle. "Poor baby."

I grab another fry and pop it into my mouth with a wink. Georgia grins. God, I've missed her. Facetiming just isn't the same. We relax into conversation and talk about our respective days. She entertains me with a story about one of the town locals, Geraldine, and her dog. As my laughter dies down, her expression grows serious.

She reaches across the table and puts a hand on mine. "Anyway, hon, how are you doing? I mean, *really* doing."

Before I can say anything, the server comes by to take our order. We both ask for burgers and Collier's Pale Ale. When he walks away, I turn back to Georgia. "Do you believe there's one special person out there for us all?"

She pauses before she speaks. "I think if we open ourselves to love, we'll find it. But is there only one person for each of us? No. I think we can love more than once." She peers at me over the rim of her glass. "Is this about Aiden?"

Just hearing his name causes me to clench my fists. I take a slow breath, and unclench my hands before shrugging because, to be honest, I'm not sure where the question came from. But I can't believe that destiny would provide someone like Aiden as my one chance at love. "Maybe."

Her expression softens. "You deserve so much better, Felix, and I know you'll find happiness again."

"What about love at first sight, then? Do you believe in that?"

Georgia scoffs. "Lust at first sight maybe, but love, not really. Why?"

Our food arrives before I can answer, and I pounce on it like a ravenous animal. I devour three quarters of the burger before placing it back on my plate. "Mmm, that's good. I forgot how delicious the burgers are here."

"You must be starving." She chuckles. "You just about inhaled the damn thing."

"I didn't think working in the coffee shop would be such hard work. I'm surrounded by food but hardly have any time to eat," I groan. "I expected it to be busy at certain times during the day, but it's constant."

Georgia nods. "The store has picked up, too, but I'm not complaining about more business. I think we're getting a lot more tourists in town."

Kit immediately comes to mind. I assume he's a tourist, although he doesn't look like the typical guests we get at the cabins. Our guests are usually families visiting local ranches, or small groups looking for adventure. Apart from jogging this morning, Kit doesn't look like he's dressed for outdoor pursuits. Plus, I think he's alone, and Collier's Creek seems a strange place for a solo vacation. Maybe he just likes the solitude of the cabin—

"Hey, what's going on in that brain of yours?"

My gaze flicks back to hers. "Just thinking of this guy I saw today."

Her brows raise and she sits up straighter, pushing her plate away. "Oh, do tell."

I run a hand through my hair, surprisingly reluctant to talk about Kit. He's made this strange impression on me that I can't figure out. He's a stranger. I don't know anything about the man, but I can't stop thinking about him.

"There's nothing to tell, really. Just this guy who's come into the coffee shop a few times. He piqued my interest."

She waggles her brows. "What's he like?"

I pick up my beer and take a long swallow before speaking. "That's the thing—I don't really know. Will says he's been coming in for a while but he just grabs a coffee to go, and he never dines in. Doesn't say much either. But there's something about him..." I trace a ring of condensation left on the table by my glass.

"Oh, a man of mystery? Sounds intriguing." She leans forward, eyes gleaming.

"Ridiculous is more like it. I have no why he's taking up so much space in my thoughts. I just got out of a relationship. There's no way I want another one—"

"I get it. After Aiden, you deserve some time to yourself. Time to lick your wounds. But that doesn't mean you can't notice an attractive man when you see one."

"Who says he was attractive?"

She barks a laugh. "You forget I have my spidey senses. You can't hide anything from me. Anyway, rebound relationships are a no-go, but don't rule out having a bit of fun. You've got to make the most of every opportunity in this town—we don't get many mysterious strangers who aren't just briefly passing through."

"I may not see him again."

"Well, if you do, ask him for a drink. Have a bit of fun, nothing serious. Enjoy yourself," she encourages. "And if you don't want to ask him for you, ask him for me. It's been a drought lately."

I nod and echo her laugh, although she's always been popular and I can't imagine her lacking for company. She likes playing the field and isn't ready to settle down. I narrow my gaze and study her as I finish my beer. Maybe things have changed. Maybe she's looking for something else now? Once upon a time, a forever kind of relationship was the last thing I wanted too, but breaking up with Aiden brought home just how much I liked the idea of settling down. I think I was more upset at the loss of the future life I'd envisaged us having than the loss of the guy himself.

After we finish our meal, we head outside into the cool night air. She takes my arm and we walk across the parking lot under a darkening sky, the stars just starting to make an appearance. At her car, I give her a quick hug, feeling lucky to have such an amazing friend, someone who's there through the good times and the bad.

Another reason to like being back in Collier's Creek.

She drives away, the engine noise fading into the distance, leaving me with my thoughts. Part of me is still thinking about our conversation—she's right, I'm not ready to jump into anything serious, but I also refuse to hide myself away and wallow. The other part is thinking of Kit.

On the drive home, I can't help wonder if I'll run into him again soon. I'm not sure if that's something I want or something that scares the living daylights out of me.

I notice how it's quieter out here, the sky darker, the stars brighter. There's a glow in the distance—the light in Kit's cabin. I tear my eyes away and force myself into my cabin, where I shower and get ready for bed. It's not so easy to force him from my thoughts as I lie under the covers and wait for sleep to come.

CHAPTER FIVE

Kit

Sitting on the swing seat after my run has become my favorite way to start the day. There's something invigorating about breathing the fresh air while sipping my coffee and contemplating the day ahead. It's taken a few days to settle into the different pace of life, but astonishingly, the words are flowing—not a torrent, more a trickle, but enough to give me hope that I'll get the damn cozy mystery book finished.

I lift the mug to my lips and gaze at the landscape. The deer hasn't made a reappearance, but the birds are in abundance. In fact, the rustle of leaves and bird calls are the only sounds until a car starts nearby. It's coming from the next cabin along. I haven't seen whoever is staying there apart from a fleeting glance through the window on my run last week. The car drives off early each morning, leaving me to the solitude I was craving when I found this place. I watch the taillights of the sedan disappear along the gravel driveway, then haul myself up and head inside.

The morning passes in a blur of words and before I know it, my stomach lets me know it's lunchtime. I rummage in the cupboard for a can of soup, emptying it into a saucepan and putting it on to heat. I slice and butter some bread, then grab a bowl, only to find the soup is stone cold. After checking to make sure it's turned on, it's obvious the stove burners aren't working. *Damn!* I sigh and tip the cold soup into the bowl and take it to the microwave, but it's not working either. *For fuck's sake.*

There's a number for the caretaker in a folder in the desk drawer. I call and leave a message, proud of myself for my restraint as I report the problem.

I eat peanut butter slapped on bread, and my mood plummets on par with my lunch expectations. My afternoon session of writing is dismal—once again I'm staring at the flashing curser. I sigh heavily, disappointed that I've hit a brick wall again. This is my fresh start, and the word flow didn't last. It all feels so hopeless. *Some writer I am!* My mood gets even darker when there's a knock on the door. I fling it open to see Shawn standing there with his toolbox.

"Got your message," he says, offering up a grin. "Thought I'd take a quick look, but if it's electrical, I'm not sure I'll be able to do much."

Before I can respond, he steps inside and heads to the kitchen.

"Of course it's electrical," I say, following him. I'll never get any work done with interruptions. "The stove and the microwave don't work."

He tests the toaster and the coffee machine. "Could be the fuse. I'll check it on my way out. Or maybe somethin's chewed through the wiring to the kitchen."

I shudder at the idea there might be rodents in the place.

Shawn looks up and clearly notes my distaste, chuckling. "The joys of country living," he teases. "The power in the rest of the cabin okay?"

"Yeah, I think so." I haven't even thought about the rest of the cabin—my focus is on being able to work. Checking the power to the laptop was the first thing I'd done. I can do without the stove and a few lights, but the laptop is crucial.

"That's good," he says with another of those grins. "Hopefully, it's nothing major then."

He's upbeat, and I wish I could share his positivity, but he's not the one without a working kitchen and no food delivery service. And how the hell will I make coffee? I'll have to drag the damn machine to another room. Plus, every minute he spends in the cabin is less time I'm working on my novel. I scowl and step back to give him space as he makes his way around the kitchen.

"Oh, dear."

I tense. That can't be good. "What?"

"Looks like the fridge is on the fritz too." He's staring into the open refrigerator, at the darkened shelves. He chuckles. "Lucky there's not much to spoil."

I peer over his shoulder at the carton of eggs, block of cheese, and milk. "Yes, well, some of us don't have time to cook," I snap. *And Mark did most of the cooking.* I refuse to acknowledge the pang of sadness at the reminder of how much my life has changed. Losing Mark nearly broke me and sometimes I think it's a miracle I can even function at all. Although, from my behavior, I'm hardly a polite member of society.

He closes the fridge and turns to me, mouth opening, then closing, as if he's changed his mind about saying something. His expression clouds and I feel guilty for snapping, but then his gaze clears and he nods. "I don't much cook either. When I lost Maureen, I'd've starved if it wasn't for the constant supply of casseroles from the folks in town."

Now it's my turn to stand there with my mouth open. Is he reading me so easily or is it just a coincidence?

I finally say the words, the same ones I've heard countless times over the last two years. "I'm sorry for your loss."

"I 'preciate that." He smiles, then the moment passes, and he gets back to business.

I trail after him as he moves to check the rest of the cabin, flicking lights on and off. "Looks like everythin's working back here, and it's just the kitchen. I'll get onto the electrician."

"Okay." It's not ideal, but it'll have to do. I follow him back to the front door. "Thanks."

"Not a problem. That's what I'm here for. Plus, we gotta look out for each other out here," Shawn says, his friendly grin back in place. "Well, you just holler if you need anythin' else."

I'm relieved as I watch him descend the porch steps with his toolbox and head around the side of the cabin. I know he means well, and he's just looking out for me, but solitude suits me so much better these days than spending time with people.

THE DAY DRAGS ON with little progress on my novel. I shove up from the desk in frustration and push open the window to let the afternoon breeze flow into the room. It's cool, but hopefully the fresh air will clear my head. Then, needing a change, I pick up one of the notebooks I bought during my last visit into town and cross to the sofa. The urge to work on my romance story is strong. There's joy in creating complex and broken characters and giving them the happy ending I never experienced. I settle back into the cushions, notebook on my lap. As the afternoon passes, I lose myself in my writing, inspired by the romantic storyline and the world of my characters.

A knock at the door startles me back to reality.

For a moment, I'm tempted to ignore it, but Shawn knows I'm home and my Jeep's still parked outside. I sigh, put down my notebook, and head to the door, flexing my chilled fingers as I do so.

"Shaw—"

It's not Shawn. It's Felix. Felix, who I dreamt about last night with his mop of wavy blond hair and warm brown eyes.

"Hey there," he says, flashing a megawatt smile. "Sorry to bother you, but Uncle Shawn asked me to drop this off." He holds up an electrical cord.

"Uncle Shawn?"

"Yep. He's the caretaker." His brows draw together. "He was here earlier today. He said you're having electrical troubles."

"Electrical troubles? Oh, right. Of course. I just wasn't expecting you."

Felix chuckles. "I'm sure you weren't."

"Sorry, I didn't know he was your uncle. But you didn't have to do this. I could have come to the main house and picked it up."

"It's no trouble. That's what neighbors are for."

"Neighbor? You live with your uncle?"

He shakes his head, indicating to the right. "I'm in the next cabin."

"The next cabin?"

Amusement is clear on Felix's face. "Are you going to echo everything I say?"

God, I'm an idiot. What is it about him that has me flustered? My stomach is in knots as he stands there with a grin on his face. I can't believe that Felix is staying in the cabin next door. The one person I'm trying to get out of my head and he's living a stone's throw away. I ignore his question and hold out my hand. "Thanks for the cord."

"No worries," he says, but he doesn't hand it over. "I promised Uncle Shawn I'd make sure it was all set up okay. The fridge is old and heavy, so you'll need a hand to plug it in."

"Fine." I step back and let him in.

Felix glances at the living area as we pass through to the kitchen. "Are you okay here? Got everything you need?"

"Everything apart from a working kitchen," I say drily.

He chuckles again, not put off by my tone. "It's just that it's a little cold in here."

I look back at the living area. I probably should have turned on a lamp or two as the sun has dropped low in the sky and sunlight is no longer streaming through the window. The only thing streaming into the room is the now-frigid air that's billowing the drapes.

"I like the fresh air while I work," I say, realizing how ridiculous that sounds. The temperature inside must have dropped twenty degrees while my story consumed me.

"Okkaay." He obviously doesn't believe me as he draws out the word, one brow raised as he studies me, a half-smile on his face. "I'd be happy to show you how to set the fire."

I fold my arms and lean against the counter. "How about you stick to fixing the fridge?"

The smile disappears. I instantly regret my blunt response. It's just that he has me on edge. I'm not used to the feelings Felix arouses with his sunshiny smile and flashing dimple, and have no idea how to process them. I'm off kilter, and I need him out of here so I can recover my equilibrium.

"Right, let's get to it then," he says, turning to the fridge. "This extension cord should reach the outlet in the other room."

He was right—the fridge is a dinosaur, and it takes the two of us to maneuver it slowly, inch by inch, from the wall so we can access the outlet. Felix's sweater pulls tight as he moves, showcasing defined biceps and muscular shoulders. He's lean, but fit. I look away. He must be in his mid-twenties—way too young for me to be ogling.

Soon the fridge is humming away, and a reprieve is in sight. Blessed solitude will be mine again—no more gorgeous young man to remind me that my best days are behind me. I walk Felix to the door. "Thanks for helping with the fridge."

"Anytime," he says. "I'm just sorry the power is a problem at all. It's not the kind of experience we want for our guests."

I'm tempted to ask him more about his connection to the cabins and his job at the coffee shop, but I bite my tongue.

There's no point getting involved. "It's fine. So long as I can charge the laptop, I'm golden."

"You're on a working vacation?" Felix asks.

"Something like that." I open the door.

"All right, I'll leave you to it then," he says, taking the hint. "Be sure to stop by CC's tomorrow and the coffee's on the house."

"You don't have to do that, it's not necessary."

"I know." His smile is bright, despite me being an asshole earlier. "See ya, Kit."

Before I can say anything else, he spins on his heel and disappears into the dusk. I'm strangely despondent as he does exactly what I want, and leaves me alone.

CHAPTER SIX

Felix

I wake slowly. Judging from the dim light filtering into the room, it's just past dawn. For a moment I'm disoriented, the silence a contrast to the usual sounds of morning traffic. Then I remember where I am and stretch with contentment—no morning rush to get to the office. It's only been a few weeks, but coming to Collier's Creek has been just the break I've needed.

With a sudden burst of energy, I roll from the bed, eager to start my day. It doesn't take long to shower and pull on jeans, a long-sleeved T-shirt, and a pair of Vans. I don't miss office attire and leather shoes for a moment.

The kitchen is chilly, but I'm not stopping long—just long enough for a quick breakfast, so I'm prepared when I'm run off my feet later. Things are a lot busier at CC's than Cam said they'd be before he left. I can't take any credit for the uptick in customers, but I'm sure he'll be happy on his return.

Warm bowl of instant oats in hand, I stand by the side window and check outside.

It's early, and Kit's cabin is quiet. Is he still in bed asleep, or is he already out on his run? I huff a laugh at my foolishness in hoping for a glimpse of him.

I try to justify my interest as appreciation because he's smoking hot, but there's something else apart from his good looks that's captured my attention. He has this brooding intensity that pulls me to him like a moth to a flame. He's not exactly the friendliest of guys, but I want to know more about him. I want to discover what secrets lie beneath his stony exterior. I want to crack that shell, and maybe earn myself a smile. I sigh as I rinse the bowl and leave it in the sink. Georgia says I'm always looking for a good cause, and I'm sure Kit, no matter how sad he looks, has no desire to be my pet project.

A short while later, I'm walking through the doors of CC's looking forward to a day of serving the fine people of Collier's Creek.

I flip on the lights and the music, and turn on the coffee machine before heading out back. I accept the early morning deliveries of milk and fresh baked goods, and stock the fridges and display cabinet. The menu focuses on simple food, like sandwiches, quiche, and lasagna, so not a lot of cooking required. Drinks and sweet treats are the most popular items. I'm putting the last of the muffins on a plate when the first customer knocks on the glass door. I set down the tongs and let them in, while flipping the sign to Open.

The morning rush picks up just as Will arrives.

"Morning, boss," he says, rounding the counter and grabbing his apron from the hook on the wall.

"Hey, Will," I say in greeting, accompanied by a roll of my eyes at the teasing way he calls me boss. We've been working well together and his easygoing manner is a breath of fresh air, unlike the atmosphere at my old job. I put the lid on the almond milk latte I've just made and pass it to the customer, as Will slides into place behind the espresso machine.

It's a busy morning. I lose myself in taking orders, prepping food, and refilling the display case. Will whips up coffee after coffee, clearing and wiping down tables between customers. We're like a well-oiled machine.

Things have finally calmed down and Will's gone on a break when the door chimes again. I glance up to see Kit walk in. My pulse increases at the sight of his piercing blue eyes.

I'm happily surprised at the brief flash of a smile he throws my way, as if manifesting my thoughts from this morning. Somehow, I know his smile is a rare thing and I'm honored to have it directed my way.

"Welcome to Coffee and Cake," I say in my brightest voice when he approaches the counter. I really must ask Cam what the Cs stand for. "What can I get for you?"

"Just coffee."

"Espresso. Double shot?"

His eyes widen, apparently surprised I remembered his coffee order. "Yeah. Thanks."

I grab the group handle and fill it with grounds. "How're the electrics?" I ask from behind the machine. He's taken out his phone and is staring at the screen. I warm when he puts it back in his jacket pocket to look at me.

"Your uncle said someone's coming around tomorrow or the next day. I can survive until then."

"Cool." The espresso machine hisses as hot water flows through the grounds. "Once again, I'm sorry for the inconvenience."

He waves a hand. "Don't be. I don't cook much anyway, so it's not really a problem."

Finished making his coffee, I don't pass it over straight away. Instead, I take a plate and load it up with a huge slice of carrot cake, then push the plate across the counter.

Kit raises his brows.

"You don't like carrot cake?"

"I... ah..."

"It's on the house," I say. "As an apology for all the trouble at the cabin."

"I don't—"

"Yeah, I know, it's not necessary," I say, echoing his words from the night before, "but I'd like you to have it. It's the best carrot cake in town."

A small smile tugs at the corner of his mouth. "If it's the best, how can I say no?"

He picks up the plate and I hand over his espresso. Our fingers touch—just a small graze, but electrifying. From the way he looks at me, I wonder if he feels it too. The noise of the coffee shop fades into the distance. It's just me and Kit, eyes locked.

That is until Georgia breaks the spell. "Well, look who we have here."

We turn our heads in unison, but before I can open my mouth, Kit speaks.

"Hi, Georgia."

"Morning, Kit." She's bright and bubbly, eyes flicking between us.

"You two know each other?" I ask.

"Sure do," Georgia says. "Kit and I go way back. Right, Kit?" She winks at Kit, who obviously has no idea how to respond to her teasing. "Actually, I haven't seen you in the store the last few days. You haven't run out of soup yet?"

"Still a can or two left," he deadpans. He faces me again. "Thanks for the cake."

I watch him head to a table on the far side of the coffee shop near the window, heart jumping a little when he takes a seat.

"Hey, Earth calling Felix." Georgia waves a hand in front of my face. "Oh, you have it bad!"

"What?' I ask, eyes snapping back to her.

"So, Kit is the guy you were talking about at dinner? The man of mystery?" she says in a low voice then sighs. "I see the attraction. He's got that sexy older man vibe going on."

I have to agree there. Today he's rocking dark growth along his jaw, the stubble giving him a slightly rough edge. The blue of his sweater makes his eyes pop and draws my gaze. I tear my eyes away, and lower my voice to match hers, although I don't think he can hear us from where he's sitting. "I have no idea if he's into men or not—"

"Oh, he's into men all right."

"How do you know?"

"Oh, hon, I saw the way he was looking at you. I'd say he's got a thing for sweet young things."

"Who's looking at who?" Will asks as he comes in from the back, overhearing us even as we're whispering.

Georgia inclines her head to where Kit is sitting. She holds a finger to her lips. "Shhh. Our Felix has a crush on Mr. Tall, Dark, and Mysterious over there."

Will glances across. "He's here. That's unusual. He usually grabs a coffee to go."

"I don't have a crush," I hiss.

Georgia's eyebrows reach her hairline. "Protest much?"

I glare at her. "So what? I have eyes. He's hot."

"You'll get no argument from me," Will says.

"Will! What will Colton think?" Georgia says in mock indignation.

Will shrugs. "He'll agree. We both know a good-looking man when we see one."

Will's boyfriend works at the local high school and is the very definition of sexy teacher. Will is a lucky man, and they're couple goals.

"So, what do you know about him?" I ask, because Georgia always has her finger on the pulse regarding what goes on in Collier's Creek. I start making her a caramel latte, while she spills the beans.

She keeps her voice low as if she's imparting state secrets. "He's been in town for a few weeks, he's staying at the cab—Wait!" she hisses. "He's *staying* at the *cabins*! Felix Montgomery, you've been holding out on me."

I chuckle. "I only met him properly last night and I haven't seen you since then. Also, there's nothing much to tell. He's staying there by himself and it looks like he's working, not on vacation."

"What sort of work?" Will asks.

"I have no idea. I just saw the laptop setup and a whole pile of papers." I press the lid on the coffee cup.

Georgia takes the latte. "You've been inside the cabin with him?"

"Hold your horses. I was dropping off an extension cord."

"And?"

"And nothing. He was a bit pissed I was there. I guess I was interrupting whatever it was he was working on, not to mention there was no power to the kitchen. Anyway," I look at her pointedly, "don't you have a store to get back to?"

She looks at her watch and scowls. "Damn, you're right, but this conversation isn't over. See you later, boys." She nods at Will and me and heads to the door. "Bye, Kit," she calls, waving at him.

Kit lifts his head and hesitantly raises a hand to wave her goodbye. It's as if he's not used to the friendliness of strangers. The door closes after her, and Kit's gaze drops back to the plate in front of him.

"He's a little like a fish out of water, isn't he?" Will says, picking up a cloth and wiping the counter. "I wonder what his story is?"

"He seems sad and lonely."

Kit forks up a piece of carrot cake and raises it to his mouth. A little cream cheese frosting sticks to his lip and his tongue flashes pink as he swipes it away.

"Here." Will nudges me and passes me a napkin from the dispenser.

"What's that for?" I ask.

"To wipe the drool from your chin."

I chuckle, but he's right. I think watching Kit eat cake is my new favorite thing.

Kit's gaze flicks toward Will and me, and I blush at being caught staring. I snatch the cloth from Will's hand and start polishing the counter as if my life depended on it. Will's laugh echoes as he disappears back into the kitchen.

CHAPTER SEVEN

Kit

The porch swing creaks as I gently rock back and forth, taking in the view. There are trees as far as the eye can see, and in the distance, the mountains rise majestically against the sky. I close my eyes and breathe in the crisp, pine-scented air. Footsteps on the gravel driveway cause me to open my eyes.

Shawn approaches with a friendly wave. "Mornin', Kit. Just wanted to let ya know the electrician will be by later to fix the issues in the kitchen."

I nod. "Thanks for arranging that."

Shawn glances at the trees. "Quite the view, huh? My Maureen, God rest her soul, loved sitting out here. Said it was the most peaceful place on earth." A wistful look crosses his face, and I feel a pang in my chest for his loss.

"It's a special place you've got here."

"That it is." His smile is back. "Been in the family for generations."

"It must be difficult managing on your own."

Shawn shrugs. "It was easier when Brian and Susan were here—"

"Brian and Susan?"

"Sorry." He chuckles. "I forget not everyone knows everyone around here. Susan's my sister and Brian's her husband.

They're Felix's parents. Moved to Florida, oh, two years ago or there abouts."

At the mention of Felix, my pulse quickens. The way he insisted I take the piece of cake, our fingers touching, his eyes on me while I sat in the coffee shop. The hint of desire I could see in his expression.

"Well, I better get to it," Shawn says, snapping me from my thoughts. "Gotta deliver some firewood to your woodpile round the back before the rain comes." I thank him as he turns to leave, my mind already wandering back to thoughts of Felix.

I head inside but have no desire to sit down at the desk. I'm tempted to visit CC's, and although it's lunchtime, I don't even try to tell myself it's for any reason other than catching a glimpse of Felix. Before I can talk myself out of it, I'm in the Jeep and on the way to town.

The bell chimes overhead as I step inside the now-familiar coffee shop. Behind the counter, Will greets me with a friendly nod. The disappointment it's not Felix behind the counter is replaced by a strange sense of belonging when Will remembers my order. He picks up a takeout cup, but I stop him. "I'll have it here today."

He smirks as he swaps the cardboard cup for a ceramic mug. "Did you want something to eat?"

My gaze flicks around the coffee shop, hoping to catch sight of Felix, but he's nowhere to be seen. However, I live in hope and decide to stay.

I turn back to Will. "I'll take a chicken salad sandwich."

Will nods. "Grab a seat. I'll bring it over."

I make my way to a small table near the front windows and pull my notepad from my pocket. I carry it with me everywhere, scrawling notes and ideas. I tried making notes on my phone but old-fashioned pen and paper suits me best.

Through the window, I watch the happenings in town. An elderly man tipping his hat at a woman walking past; a young man pushing a stroller; a teenager engrossed in something on her phone. Will brings my food and I stop people-watching as I bite into my sandwich. It feels strange to be out and about instead of doing chores and rushing straight home. The sandwich is better than anything I could throw together and I enjoy the change in routine. I sip the coffee, needing the bitter jolt of caffeine—I've been burning the candle at both ends trying to get this damn book written. I tune out the murmur of conversation and review the list in my notebook, contemplating my latest idea for a red-herring.

Out of the corner of my eye, I catch a flash of blond hair. Felix is crossing the room with a tray. Our eyes meet and he gives me a little wave before heading to a table and clearing the dishes. I like the view as he leans across to pick up a milkshake glass, the apron he wears framing his pert ass. His jeans mold to his body, showing off a gorgeous bubble-butt. I flush and stare down at my notepad, suddenly self-conscious.

Jesus! I need to pull myself together.

Still, I can't help tracking him around the coffee shop as he clears empty mugs and wipes down tables. He's at ease with the regulars, stopping to chat, eyes crinkling as he laughs. It's clear he loves his job and that the locals love him.

As he heads back to the counter, he glances my way. I offer a small smile, then pretend to be engrossed in my notes. My sandwich sits half-eaten thanks to the butterflies in my stomach. The physical reaction surprises me—I haven't felt anything like this for... for I don't know how long. I doodle in the margins of my notebook as I try to analyze what the hell is happening to me. I haven't come to any conclusions when footsteps approach and Felix is by my table, juice and a slice of pie in hand.

"Mind if I join you?" he asks.

I automatically gesture to the empty seat across from me. "Please."

He places the pie in front of me, then settles in, sitting back and sipping his juice.

I glance from the pie to Felix. "For me?"

"It didn't look as if you were enjoying the sandwich. I thought this might be more tempting." He takes another sip of juice, lips pursed around the straw. My thoughts take a dive into the gutter, imagining those lips doing obscene things. He's temptation personified.

I swallow heavily. "Thanks." A small dimple flashes as he smiles. "I... um... have you worked here long?"

"Actually, no," he replies. "Just a few weeks. A friend asked me to manage the place while he was away for a few months, but to be honest, it's been a refreshing change."

"Yeah? What is it you usually do?"

"The last couple of years, I've been an executive assistant to a department head at a menswear retail chain." He must sense my surprise and chuckles. He hooks a thumb under the leather strap of his apron and gives it a tug. "Not exactly high fashion, is it?"

"So why the change?" I ask, then realize I'm being nosy. "Just ignore me. You don't have to answer that."

He waves a hand. "It's cool. I had a messy breakup. I made the mistake of dating someone I worked with. Unfortunately, he fucked his way up the corporate ladder, starting with my boss."

"Jesus!"

Felix raises a brow. "Sorry, that was probably TMI."

It sounds like he was well and truly fucked over, and I'm surprised he's so upbeat about it, but I'm also a little pleased at the use of pronouns. "That's messed up," I say, offering a sympathetic smile.

"You can say that again. But onward and upward. I'm better off without that kind of shit in my life." He sits up straighter. "You know, the most surprising thing about it all is how much I'm enjoying being back in Collier's Creek and working here at CC's. How are you liking our little town so far?"

"More than I thought I would."

Felix laughs. "If you thought you wouldn't like it, why on earth did you come?"

I look at him and wonder how much to share. I came here for anonymity, amongst other things. However, I find myself opening up. "I wanted to escape the city. I was looking for someplace secluded with limited distractions."

"And how's that working out for you?" he asks, twirling his straw in his now-empty glass, a flirtatious twinkle in his eye.

I wonder if he's asking what I think he's asking. I clear my throat. "At least the cabin's fairly remote," I say.

His lip twitches as he holds back a smile. "And why Collier's Creek?"

"Ahh." I chuckle. "There wasn't much thought involved. Ten minutes on the internet was all it took. I looked for somewhere far enough away that I wouldn't be easily tempted to drive home to Seattle. Plus, Collier's Creek sounded idyllic. I imagined a picturesque town with a river and mountains in the distance—blue skies and trees as far as the eye can see. So far, it's delivered on that promise."

"It is like a postcard," Felix agrees. "I grew up here and it was exciting to escape small town life, but as I've gotten older, I've come to appreciate the lifestyle more. Like I said, it's good to be back. It's home, you know?"

I chuckle at his reference to getting older. He must be all of twenty-three or twenty-four. "Were you away long?"

"A few years. I'm twenty-four," he says, answering my unasked question. "What about you? Are you planning to head back home to Seattle soon?"

Surprisingly, I'm oddly disturbed by the thought of leaving. I feel as if I'm just getting my footing and I'm not ready to resume my old life, rattling around a house that's way too big for one person. I shake my head. "No plans yet."

"You're working from here?" Felix asks.

"I am. Luckily I have the type of job that means I can work from pretty much anywhere, so long as I have my laptop and Wi-Fi."

The bell on the door jingles as Logan from the bookstore enters and holds the door open for Mrs. Hendricks. They make their way to the counter, the elderly lady chatting non-stop. She hardly pauses for breath as they give their orders to a bemused Will.

"Logan's a regular here," Felix says, noticing me looking their way. "He works at the bookstore next door. I'm sure you've probably seen her around too."

I nod. "The bookstore is fantastic. And yes, I've met Mrs. Hendricks."

"It's hard not to run into everyone in a small town."

"Is that one of the good qualities, or the bad?" I ask.

Felix chuckles. "It depends on the day and who you ask."

Logan waves as he makes eye contact, then settles at a nearby table. Mrs. Hendricks places her over-sized purse on a spare chair and delves into its depths, dragging out a paperback that she places on the table. They're too far away for me to see what she's reading, but from her animation, it's obvious they're discussing the novel.

"I'd better get back to work," Felix says. "Break's over."

My gaze flicks to his as he pushes up from his chair. "Enjoy the pie."

I realize I haven't eaten a bite, too caught up in our all-too-brief discussion. I smile in thanks and pick up my fork as he walks away. The pie is delicious and I savor each mouthful as I watch Felix back in action behind the counter. Then the couple at the nearby table catch my attention.

Logan and Mrs. Hendricks are talking, heads close. Mrs. Hendricks stabs at the back of the book as if making a point. She looks at me, then back at Logan, still talking a mile a minute but in low tones. I can't hear a word of the conversation. Logan's gaze meets mine and a tingle of nervous energy creeps over me as my heart skips a beat. Then Logan smiles, a genuine smile that makes me think I was reading too much into his stare. *God, I need to relax.* I blink away the discomfort and let out a slow breath, regaining my composure.

The pleasure I'd felt earlier slips away. As warm and inviting as the coffee shop is, and as much as I've loved the interaction with Felix, there are always risks when venturing out into the world, even in Collier's Creek.

I close my notebook, rise from the table, and make my way to the counter.

"Heading out already?" Felix asks.

Is that a flicker of disappointment I see in his eyes?

I nod. "I need to get back to my work."

He rings me up. I hand him some bills, our fingers brushing for the briefest moment.

"I hope I'll see you tomorrow," he says.

"We'll see." I turn to leave.

"Kit. Wait."

I stop in my tracks, turning to face him again. "Yeah?"

"I was wondering if you'd like to join me for dinner tomorrow night?"

My heart misses a beat. "I don't know—"

"You can't tell me you have other plans because I know you don't know anyone, or at least I think you don't. Plus, I'm all alone out there. Seems a shame not to share a meal. You wouldn't deny me an hour or so of your time, would you?" He flutters his eyelashes.

I can't help smiling. He's totally irresistible and impossible to say no to. I guess a simple dinner can't hurt. "Okay. That sounds nice."

His grin is wide. "Good. It's a date."

A date. I know it's just an expression but I wish—no! "See you tomorrow," I say.

I turn and hurry to the door, but not before catching Mrs. Hendricks' stare.

I head back to the cabin. At least there I know I don't have to worry about prying eyes.

CHAPTER EIGHT

Felix

The timer startles me from my daydream. I pull the casserole from the oven, the savory aroma of beef and vegetables filling the small cabin. I'm not sure what's come over me, but I'm imagining life back here in Collier's Creek. There's a lot to be done around here and my head's filled with a list of things I'd like to do. I imagine the cabins as they were in their heyday, before time and Dad's health decline took their toll. But my stay here is meant to be temporary; I'll have to work on a plan and figure out a way to help Uncle Shawn when I'm gone.

I glance around, ensuring everything is in place—the table set, the cushions plumped, a fire crackling away in the fireplace. I change the playlist on my phone so that soft music fills the space. Maybe the change in pace will help calm the nervous energy that courses through me as I wait Kit's arrival.

I've been thinking about him all day, our conversation from yesterday replaying in my mind. The way he focused on me, his smile. Maybe it's just lust, but I felt a connection, an attraction that's impossible to ignore.

A knock at the door jolts me back. I take a deep breath, trying to slow my racing heart. Opening the door, I'm momentarily speechless seeing Kit standing there. He's wearing a jacket over dark jeans, paired with a gray knit sweater with a zip at the throat. The short scruff along his jaw has been trimmed and his dark hair swept back from his forehead. He's so GQ cover worthy, I almost groan.

"Hey! I'm so glad you could make it," I say, trying to appear cool as I step aside. "Come on in."

Kit enters, glancing around. I try to see the cabin through his eyes. Homely? Rustic? A little tired?

"Something smells amazing." He holds out a bottle of red wine.

"Just a beef and veggie casserole. And thanks, this looks great," I say, accepting the wine.

"Thanks for having me over. It's been a while since I've had a home-cooked meal."

"It's nice to have the company. Make yourself comfortable."

He shrugs off his jacket and I hang it on the hook near the door, then take the wine to the kitchen counter and hunt for a corkscrew. "Did you have a productive day?" I ask as I open another drawer and rummage through the utensils.

"I didn't get as much done as I would have liked, but things are progressing."

I look up to see him standing in front of the fireplace, holding his hands to the warmth. The shadows of his cheekbones are accentuated by the flickering flames. He flicks his gaze to mine and I immediately duck my head, delving back into the drawer. "There should be one in here somewhere," I mutter.

When I next look up, Kit is standing nearby. "I assume you don't drink a lot of wine," he says with a wry grin.

"What gives it away?"

He laughs, a proper laugh that comes from somewhere deep inside him, and just like that, I relax.

"Do you like beer?" I ask. "Or there's a bottle of whiskey around here somewhere."

"Too much of anything is bad, but too much good whiskey is barely enough." he responds.

I raise a brow.

"Mark Twain."

"Ahh. Got ya. So whiskey it is?"

Kit shrugs. "I'll have whatever you're having."

"Oh, I know that one! When Harry Met Sally."

Kit's laughter fills the room. "Close enough."

I grab a bottle of beer from the fridge. It's my usual Collier's Pale Ale, but I decide to mix it up a bit. I find the bottle of rye Uncle Shawn usually drinks and put both bottles onto the counter. I take two highballs and two shot glasses from the cupboard. Kit is watching my every move. "Have you ever tried a Wyoming Boilermaker?" I ask.

"I can't say that I have."

"Not exactly fine wine, but it's definitely an experience and something you should try at least once."

I push one of each of the filled glasses toward Kit, then pick up a shot glass and hold it above my beer. I encourage Kit to do the same. He looks unsure, but he follows. I drop the shot glass into the beer. It hits the bottom with a clunk and foam rises over the edge. I quickly bring it to my mouth and manage to swallow a few mouthfuls, foam dripping down my chin.

Kit throws his drink back. He puts the empty glass down with a thud. "Holy shit! That's horrible."

"Not a fan of the bomb shot?" I ask as I tip the rest of my drink down the sink and wipe my mouth with the back of my hand.

He rolls his eyes, but I notice his gaze drop to my mouth. I run my tongue along my bottom lip, tasting the hops and alcohol and wish I was tasting him instead.

Kit is the first to break the tension. He clears this throat. "Can I give you a hand with dinner?"

"Sure."

Together we dish up the casserole and soon we're seated opposite each other at the small table.

"This is really good," Kit says after a few bites. "Where did you learn to cook this like?"

"My mom. You may have noticed there isn't much in the way of home delivery here, so we ate a lot of home-cooked meals. She taught me most of her recipes. I think she secretly wanted a daughter but had to make do with me."

"Perhaps she's just equal opportunity?" Kit says.

I shrug. "Maybe, but my folks are pretty much set in their gender roles. Mom did most of the house stuff, and Dad took care of the outdoors."

"Shawn said they've retired. To Florida?"

I finish my mouthful before answering. "Dad's health was bad for a few years, then he had an injury to his back. It became too hard for him to do the repair work around here and manage chores like chopping firewood. Uncle Shawn had been away for ten years, but came back to lend a hand, then convinced them it was his turn to put in the hard work so they could retire to a warmer climate."

"You weren't tempted to follow in the family footsteps?" Kit asks.

"To Florida?"

Kit chuckles. "No, managing the cabins."

I sigh and put down my fork. "Now that's a long story."

"I've got time," he says. "If you want to tell it."

"How about the short version?" I get up and grab us a couple of bottles of beer—no whiskey this time—and slide one across to Kit. "Growing up in Collier's Creek was amazing. What kid wouldn't want to be able to fish, and hike, and run wild through the mountains?"

He looks at me and nods. "Sounds idyllic."

"It was." I take a long sip of ale as I remember my teenage years. "Don't get me wrong, it was hard work too. I was expected to do chores after school and study hard, but I couldn't imagine a better life. I wanted nothing more than to work alongside Dad or maybe open a store. Not big plans, just enough, you know?"

Kit pushes his plate away and leans his forearms on the table. "I sense a but."

"But Mom and Dad wanted more for me. I'm their only child. They both worked so hard to give me the opportunities they never had. They encouraged me to want to try new things, to have bigger dreams."

"They didn't want you to take over the family business?"

"Not exactly. They just wanted me to experience the world first, get an education, and make sure it was something I absolutely wanted to do."

"And did you?"

"Did I experience the world?"

"Did you find your path in life?"

Now that's the million-dollar question. I take a moment to think about my response. "At first I couldn't wait to move away—I was going to conquer the world. I moved to the city, studied business administration at college, then started my career. I enjoyed what I was doing, but I don't think my job was ever an all-consuming passion." I take a sip of my drink. "To be honest, now that I'm home, I don't even miss it." *Wow!* I shock myself with that thought, suddenly feeling light as I acknowledge the truth of my feelings.

"Do you like working at the coffee shop?"

"I do." My heart warms at how I spend my days. "I like dealing directly with our customers, very different from working in the corporate office. I've also discovered I like working for myself."

We continue talking about CC's, then touch on some of the ideas I've had for this place. Before long, our bottles are drained and we clear away the dishes. It's surprisingly easy to talk to Kit, and I don't want the evening to end. I don't think he does either as he readily accepts the offer of coffee.

We move to the couch in front of the fire with our mugs. This time it's me asking the questions. I want to know what he does, to learn more about him.

"You mentioned you can do your job from anywhere. What is it you do?"

There's a slight shift in his body language. It's subtle, but I can see he's reluctant to answer my question. "I'm a writer," he eventually says.

"That's awesome," I say. "I don't think I've ever met a writer before. Have you written anything I'd know?"

He shrugs. "That depends. Do you read?"

"The last novel I read was a Zane Grey Uncle Shawn gave me. He's a fan of westerns." I tilt my head and tap my chin. "You're not Zane Grey are you?"

Kit laughs, his whole face lighting up. "Thankfully not, or I'd be dead. And westerns aren't my thing."

"What is your thing?"

"Mysteries," he replies before bringing his mug to his mouth.

I can't help chuckling, earlier conversations about Kit echoing in my mind.

He raises a brow.

"Mr. Tall, Dark, and Mysterious," I say in response to the unasked question.

"I'm not following."

"It's how Georgia referred to you—"

"You were talking about me?" He frowns, dark brows drawn over his blue eyes.

I huff a laugh. "Of course. This is a small town. Everyone talks about everyone. I was telling Georgia about you—" Fuck! Now I sound like he's been on my mind. So much for playing it cool. My cheeks heat so I quickly change the subject back to him. "Anyway, are you working on anything at the moment? I saw you had a laptop open, and I've seen you scribbling away in the notebook."

He looks to the fire for a moment, then turns back with a half-smile. "The words aren't exactly flowing right now."

"Writer's block?"

Kit nods. "I was hoping the change of scene and lack of interruptions would be good for my creativity."

"And it's not working?"

He ponders for a moment, as if he's weighing up his response. "I've started a new romance novel."

"Really?"

"Don't look so surprised. There's a lot of inspiration around here." He holds my gaze, his voice gravelly.

Is he flirting? I want to retort with something witty, maybe test the waters, so to speak, but words fail me. "What's your story about?"

"Broken hearts and second chances."

"It sounds sad."

"Ah, but it's a romance." Kit smiles and relaxes against the couch, arm slung along the back, fingers toying with the fringe of the blanket folded there. "The story is guaranteed a happily ever after."

I angle myself to face him, one foot tucked under my butt. He talks more about his story, becoming animated as he describes his characters. It sounds as if he's talking about friends, not fictional people. He's obviously passionate about writing, and I'm equally drawn to Kit and the love story he's bringing to life. I could listen to him talk all night.

"And so," he finishes up, "there'll be a grand gesture toward the end and our hero will get his man."

"A happy ending," I murmur. I look to the fire; the logs are glowing red, the flames flickering low, no longer roaring. There's a heaviness in my chest as I think of how hard some people have to fight for their happiness.

"Hey, are you okay?"

I turn back to him. "Just thinking of some not so happy endings. It's a shame real life isn't like a rom com. Sometimes we have to go through so damn much just to get the happy ending we deserve."

"Speaking from experience?" Kit asks. I can see the sympathy in his eyes.

I shrug. "I was cheated on, but I'll get over it. I was thinking more of Cameron, my friend who owns the coffee shop. He's travelling with his boyfriend at the moment. They nearly didn't make it. They'd only just got back together when Greg had an accident. It was touch and go there for a while. I can't think of anything worse."

Kit nods slowly. "Losing someone you love is hard."

I can see it written on his face—the sadness. I place a hand on his thigh. "I'm sorry."

He offers a small smile, just a quick upturn of his mouth. "Sometimes opening yourself up to possibilities is harder still."

I swallow heavily at his words. Does he mean...?

He places his hand lightly over mine and a spark of electricity travels up my arm. Our eyes lock and time stands still. I search his face, looking to see he wants this as much as me. His thumb brushes across the top of my hand. I lean in slowly, heart pounding. Kit meets me halfway, his lips finding mine in a soft, tentative kiss. Warmth spreads through me at the contact. It's a barely-there kiss that hints at so much more.

We break apart for a moment, breaths mingling. Then we come together again, the kiss deepening, mouths opening to each other. His stubble scrapes my chin. I reach up and run my fingers through his hair as we press closer. It's awkward with the way we're positioned on the couch, but I don't want to stop to get comfortable. His tongue darts along my bottom lip, then delves inside to touch mine. He tastes of coffee and I can't get enough. Kit's arms wrap around me and pull me closer. He's bigger than me, broader, and I groan at being against his hard chest, held in place with strong arms.

The fire pops as a log explodes, and I flinch.

Kit pulls back abruptly. There's panic in his eyes. He runs a hand through his hair, confusion and fear etched on his face.

"I'm sorry, I... I can't do this," he stammers.

Before I can say a word, he's on his feet, heading for the door and grabbing his coat.

"Kit, wait!" I call out, rushing after him, but he's already disappeared into the darkness.

The frigid air dances around me as I stand there, stunned. Eventually, I close the door and lean against it, my fingers touching my still-tingling lips in disbelief. What just happened? One moment we were kissing as if our lives depended on it, the next he couldn't get away from me fast enough.

Chapter Nine

Kit

I didn't sleep a wink, tossing and turning with thoughts of Felix and the disastrous ending to the night swirling in my mind. The kiss... it was unexpected, surprising. I've kept my emotions reined in for so long, it was overwhelming.

The morning air is cold against my skin as I step outside, the steaming mug of coffee doing little to warm my numb fingers. I stare into the distance.

I've been afraid to let anyone in, not wanting to put myself through heartache again. I don't think I could survive having my heart ripped out again. But Felix's smile, his laugh, his positivity—the way his eyes light up when he talks about this town and the people he cares about—it chips away at my defenses, makes me want to open up again. He makes me want to try, but self-preservation kicked in. As soon as our lips touched, panic seized me and I ran.

Felix didn't deserve that. My freakout must have left him confused as hell. After all, he was just doing the neighborly thing and inviting me for a meal. There's a definite attraction, and I'm sure he was up for making out, but I'm sure he didn't expect to have to deal with my issues. I owe him an explanation.

With a sigh, I sink into the porch swing, the old wood creaking under my weight. My free hand encounters an unexpected softness and I look down to see a folded blanket on the seat next to me. It's the same blanket that was draped over the back of Felix's couch, a soft knit in alternating stripes of blue and white. I carefully pull it across my lap and run my fingers over the wool as a smile tugs at my lips. Even after I fled last night, he still thought of my comfort. That has to be a good sign, right?

My eyes are drawn to his cabin, where his sedan is gone from its usual spot. He must have already left for the day. Part of me is thankful I don't have to face him yet, but at the same time I'm disappointed. I definitely owe him an apology.

My fingers curl around the warm mug, soaking up its heat. I take a sip. As the coffee warms me from the inside out, and the blanket shields me from the chilly air, my thoughts drift back to last night. Felix's lips were so soft, tentative at first, but gaining courage. He kissed me with a tenderness I haven't felt in years—haven't allowed myself to feel. A tenderness I thought was lost forever. But maybe, just maybe, there's still hope for me yet.

THE BELL CHIMES AS I push open the door of CC's. A few of the customers glance at me as I enter, but I ignore them. I immediately spot Felix behind the counter, sorting through a folder of paperwork. He glances up, surprise flashing across his face before his signature smile appears.

"Hey, Kit," he says, closing the folder. "Wasn't sure if I'd see you today."

I rub the back of my neck, nerves getting the better of me. No point putting it off. "Yeah, about last night—"

Felix holds up a hand. "Don't. It's okay. I get it."

His easy-going manner catches me off guard. I stare at him for a moment. Maybe he doesn't need an explanation, but he certainly deserves an apology.

Before I can respond, the door opens again, and a group of chattering women enter, followed by Logan.

"Hello, Felix, dear," Mrs. Hendricks says as she stops on her way past. "We just had the most interesting discussion about a romance novel Georgia recommended. Much more risque than I'm used to. I need a tea to calm my nerves. Please send over a pot immediately."

Georgia rolls her eyes dramatically. "Oh poppycock, Mrs. Hendricks. You know you loved every minute."

The other ladies laugh as they move to the large table near the rear of the coffee shop and take their seats, Mrs. Hendricks at the head of the table.

Logan stops next to us and leans in. "Book Club," he whispers. "We meet in the bookstore, but the ladies wanted to continue their chat and hassled me to join them for lunch. Wish me luck."

"Poor Logan." Felix chuckles, then turns to me. "Why don't you join them, Kit? I'm sure you'd enjoy a discussion about romance novels. It's right up your alley."

Logan raises a brow at Felix's remark. "Another romance lover? The more the merrier. Come keep me company."

For a moment, I hesitate, but Logan's ready smile and Georgia's beckoning decide for me. What do I have to lose?

"Go on," Felix encourages. "I'll bring you your coffee."

I nod and drag over a chair, positioning myself at the edge of the group. Mrs. Hendricks treats me like a long-lost friend and introduces me to the rest of the book club members.

"So, what were you discussing today?" I ask.

"Just dissecting a steamy romance," Georgia says, her eyes full of mischief. She's one of the youngest in the small group, most of them middle-aged woman. I'm sensing she has a lot of fun interjecting her opinions and aiming for the shock factor.

"We were talking about how the author mastered the slow burn romance."

Mrs. Hendricks nods. "It was a lovely love story."

Felix comes to the table with my espresso. "Kit's a writer."

My stomach drops, but I can't blame Felix for exposing me. I never said it was a secret.

"Really?" Georgia exclaims. "What do you write?"

All eyes turn to me. I freeze for a moment, unsure what to say. Avoiding the pressure of being in the public eye is why I came to Collier's Creek and there's no way I'm exposing myself to that sort of interest again. I wave a hand. "I'm just dabbling with a romance story," I say, fudging the truth.

"Not writing the next great American novel?" Logan asks.

I huff a laugh. I can barely finish my cozy mystery, let alone write a classic.

Felix takes everyone's orders as the discussion focuses on what book to read next. We eat sandwiches, and book talk eventually turns to conversation about the latest romances in town. The ladies seem enraptured by the romance between the sheriff and a dispatcher from his office. I glance at Logan, recalling Mrs. Hendricks mentioning his boyfriend, Cooper. It seems romance is very much alive in Collier's Creek.

The book club members eventually disperse, the coffee shop quietening without their chatter. Felix wipes down the tables, humming softly to himself. I slowly get up from my seat, working up my nerve.

"Hey," I finally say, clearing my throat awkwardly as I approach him. "I wanted to say I was sorry for rushing out last night. I... I really enjoyed our time together."

"You don't owe me any explanations," Felix says, giving me a warm smile. "There's nothing to be sorry about."

I nod, exhaling in relief that he seems okay with what went down, but I disagree, I owe him more than the simple apology. "I was wondering if you'd like to come over tonight? I could cook dinner..." I trail off uncertainly. What am I saying? I can't cook to save my life, well, maybe a few breakfast dishes, but nothing that signifies an apology dinner.

Felix looks unsure, but after a moment or two where I hold my breath, he smiles. "I'd like that."

The relief is instant. "Great. I'll see you sometime after six then?"

"I'll look forward to it."

I head out the door, wondering what I've just got myself into, but happy all the same. Now I just need to figure out what to fix for dinner.

Chapter Ten

Felix

"Right on time. Come on in." Kit smiles and steps aside.

I enter the cabin, holding out a bottle of red wine. "I hear this is a good one."

Kit laughs and takes the re-gifted bottle of pinot. "Thanks."

I shrug off my coat, then follow him through to the kitchen. The makings of a salad are spread across the counter and there's a hint of garlic in the air.

Kit grabs a couple of wine glasses.

"Feeling positive?" I joke.

"Always." Kit grins as he opens one of the drawers, and to my amazement, pulls out an antique corkscrew and holds it in the air like a trophy. "It's a bitch to use, but it does the trick."

"I guess you won't be needing this, then." I pull a shiny new corkscrew from my pocket.

"Gimme that." He snatches it from my hold. "Don't think you'll be getting this back."

It's nice to share a laugh—I'm relieved there's no awkwardness between us.

We touch glasses after he pours the wine, our gazes locked. He's the first to look away, quickly taking a step back and picking up a knife.

"Why don't you take a seat while I finish up here?"

"Sure." I smile and wander over to the fireplace with my wine. The fire is abysmal, barely emitting any heat. Poorly laid, it's obviously struggling to take hold. Leaving my glass on the mantle, I pick up the poker and get to work, rearranging logs until the flames jump. The room will be warmer in no time.

"Ah, a proper country boy, I see."

I rise to see Kit placing his drink on the coffee table. I grab my glass and move to join him on the couch. "You're lucky I'm here to give you some fire pointers or else you'd freeze."

He chuckles before growing serious. "On that note, thanks for the blanket. The days are getting colder, so I appreciate it."

I warm at the acknowledgement of my small gesture.

We sit side by side watching the growing fire. It's comfortable listening to the pop and crackle of flames. There's soft music playing, some type of instrumental. We sit in silence for a few moments until finally Kit speaks.

"Listen, I know you don't think we need to talk about last night, but I want to explain."

I've already told him he doesn't owe me any explanations, but this is the second time he's brought it up, so I'll listen. "Okay."

"First, I'm sorry for running off after we... you know." He pauses to take a sip of wine. "It wasn't you."

I raise a brow in amusement.

A smile plays at his lips. "Okay, that's cliched, but really, it's me. I'm not good with people. Too much time spent alone, I guess." He runs a hand through his dark hair. "To be honest, you're probably lucky things ended like they did. I'm kind of a grumpy asshole, in case you haven't noticed."

"A little broody, maybe," I say.

He gives a wry chuckle. "That's a nice way of putting it. I'm better off alone rather than putting someone through dealing with my moods."

I watch him carefully. Under the self-deprecating humor, I sense his pain. Impulsively, I reach out and squeeze his hand.

"I like dealing with you, moods and all," I say gently.

Kit meets my gaze, surprise flickering in those blue eyes. The corner of his mouth lifts as if he's about to say something, but instead, clears his throat and stands. "I'd better check on dinner."

I follow him to the kitchen, where he takes a lasagna and some garlic bread from the oven. I sip my wine as I watch him plate up.

Not long after, he carries two plates to the small dining table where a salad already waits. "It's just a ready-made lasagna from the general store," he says with an apologetic half-smile. "I'm not much of a cook."

"Hey, a hot meal on a cold night? And one I didn't have to cook? I'll take it." I pick up my fork. "It looks and smells amazing."

We eat in silence for a few minutes. Kit is pushing the lasagna around his plate more than eating it. His brow is furrowed, lips pressed in a tight line. "Hey, there's no pressure here," I say, wanting to put him at ease. "We can get to know each other as friends. We don't need to be anything more." I say the words, but I can't deny I wouldn't be opposed to more than friendship. However, friends is better than nothing and it looks as if that's what Kit needs right now.

He visibly relaxes, the tension easing from his shoulders. "Yeah. Yeah, that sounds good." He pauses, then adds softly, "I'd like us to be friends."

"Me too," I say. And I mean it. Underneath that prickly exterior, I know there's a man there that I'd like to know, and he just needs time to open up.

"Alright then, it's settled." Kit extends his hand across the table. "Friends?"

I shake it firmly. "Friends."

His hand is warm in mine. For a moment, our eyes lock, and an undercurrent of electricity passes between us. I let go first, casually leaning back in my chair, not wanting to spook him.

"Well, friend, since you admitted you can't cook, maybe I'll bring over one of my homemade casseroles sometime," I say, lightening the mood. "I also have loads of leftovers from the coffee shop."

Kit grins. "I'd like that. Just don't tell the whole town I'm a terrible cook. I have a reputation as a fully functioning adult to maintain."

I mime locking my lips. "Your secret's safe with me."

We laugh then, the tension broken, and the rest of evening passes in relaxed conversation.

As I leave later that night, I'm hopeful. We may not be romantically involved, but I love his company and for now, friendship is enough.

I'M TAKING A DAY off. My last free day was spent working around the cabins but today it's all about pleasure. I've got a definite bounce in my step as I approach Jake's Tap. I still can't believe Kit agreed to meet for lunch given he said how under the pump he was, but I'm glad he did.

I arrive first, settling into a booth near the back. The lunch crowd is sparse, just a few regulars sitting up at the bar. I order an iced tea while I wait, sipping it slowly as I watch the door. Not long after, Kit walks in, scanning the room until he spots me. I wave and his face lights up as he heads straight over.

"Hi," he says, sliding into the booth across from me.

"Hi yourself."

We chat for a bit until the server appears and takes our orders. We continue with meaningless small talk until the food and a beer for Kit arrives. Once the server leaves, an awkward silence falls. We both take a sip of our drinks, not quite making eye contact.

I put my glass down. "So—" I begin.

"So—" Kit says at the same time.

We both laugh.

"This doesn't have to be weird," I say. "We're just two friends having lunch."

Kit leans back against the vinyl booth. "You're right."

Thankfully the conversation flows more easily after that. We eat heaped bowls of pasta and chat about books and Kit's writing. He seems a lot more serious about his writing than I first thought and even has a publisher. I'm impressed and hang on his every word. It's fascinating to hear about the publishing world. He's more relaxed, his guard lowered as he talks about the creative process and an upcoming deadline.

"Wow. You're under a lot of pressure. I thought being an author was a glamorous life. You know, typing away on an old manual typewriter in the garret of your mansion while your butler brings you tea, or maybe scribbling in a notebook while sipping on chianti overlooking an orchard in Tuscany."

Kit laughs, head thrown back. I'm transfixed by the line of his throat, and the movement of his Adam's apple. I want to reach out and touch him but stop myself. We're just friends. But the chemistry between us is undeniable. His gaze lingers on me in a way that's definitely more than friendly and makes my stomach flutter. Our eyes lock again, and I lean in instinctively. Kit's tongue darts out to wet his lips, and the urge to kiss him is overpowering—I want another taste of him.

Then the server appears to clear the table, breaking the spell.

I sit back and down the last of my iced tea, needing the cold drink to calm me down. But there's an awareness thrumming between us, a heat that's hard to ignore. I can't help wonder if this friends thing is going to work. I want it to for Kit's sake, but hell, it's going to kill me. I can't help hoping for more.

Later, as we leave the bar, I can feel eyes on us. I know word will spread fast about Kit and my lunch date despite us just being friends. Let them talk, I think defiantly, stealing a glance at Kit's profile. What we have is no one's business but our own.

LATER THAT NIGHT, I'M doing a load of laundry when the phone rings.

"Soooo, Felix," comes Georgia's familiar voice. "I heard you had lunch today at Jake's with Kit. A nice long lunch."

I sigh, sensing where this is headed. I put the washing basket on my bed. "We're just friends, Georgia."

"Mmhmm. Friends who make bedroom eyes at each other across the table."

I roll my eyes, even though she can't see me. "Come on. You know it's not like that."

"So he didn't make you dinner the other night too?"

"It was store-bought lasagna as you well know, given you most likely sold it to him," I retort. "He doesn't know anyone else in town—"

"He knows me."

I ignore her interruption. "He's staying at our cabins and I live next door. Honestly, we're just friends. I'm not saying I wouldn't be happy for more. I mean, who'd be stupid enough to kick someone like Kit out of bed? But he's not interested."

"I wouldn't be so sure about that," she says, then sighs. "Look, I know I said to find someone and have a bit of fun, but I think Kit's got baggage. I can tell you really like him, but I'm not sure he's the best person to have a casual fling with. Plus, he's a little older—"

"Age is irrelevant." I know I sound defensive, but the fact he's older doesn't bother me. To be honest, I like it. "Sure he's good looking, but it isn't just about that. He's interesting to talk to and we have a great time together. And we *are* just friends."

For now, at least.

"Okay, okay," Georgia relents. "I just want you to be happy, Felix. You deserve it."

"I am happy. Or at least I was until you started to give me a hard time. Some best friend you are."

"Alright, I'll let it go. But promise you'll be careful. I don't want to have to nurse your broken heart. I love you, honey."

"I know you're just looking out for me."

We say our goodbyes and I hang up, but Georgia's concern weighs on me. I know she means well, but she's only seen the brooding exterior Kit shows to the world. She hasn't seen the glimpses I've seen. With a sigh, I try to push her doubts from my mind before they can take root. Kit and I are just having fun getting to know each other. Sure, I want to fuck his brains out, but at the moment that's just a fantasy. What's the harm in that?

CHAPTER ELEVEN

Kit

"Come on, Kit. Give me some good news," Mike pleads.

I can hear the hopefulness in his voice and I'm pleased I can offer him some reassurance. "The drought has broken. I've drafted a couple of chapters since we last spoke."

"That's awesome," he says. "Looks like you were right about the change of scene."

I wander around the cabin as I talk, sunlight streaming through the large window overlooking the woods. It's an amazing view that always lifts my spirits. Green instead of city streets. "Collier's Creek was definitely the right choice."

"Well, whatever you're doing out there, keep it up," Mike jokes. "I'm glad things are back on track."

"Me too. It's peaceful here. Quiet. Just what I need."

"Hold on a sec."

I can hear Mike typing as I cross to the window near the desk. Felix's cabin is in the distance. He's outside, grabbing something from his car. I watch him for a while and smile so hard my cheeks hurt. I can't help it. Just the sight of him makes me happy.

"Okay. Got it," Mike says, interrupting my reverie. "Says here there's a bookstore in Collier's Creek. Ellis Books. I'll get in touch with them and arrange a signing."

I grasp the phone tightly. "You'll what?"

"It's time you got back out there, Kit. Your readers will forget about you."

My blood pressure rises. "That's bullshit. For a start, my readers won't forget about me. My royalties prove it."

"We need to drum up some publicity," Mike insists. "It's been nearly two years. You should be…" His words die off.

My body tenses as heat flushes through my veins. "What? I should be over losing Mark? I should have put everything behind me by now?" How dare he! I resist the urge to pound the window sill.

"Okay, okay, I'm sorry. But listen, Kit, you can't hide away forever. You have talent and people want to read your work, and they want to know more about the man behind the words, not just buy the books."

"And that's what I don't want. Christ, Mike! There was so much speculation after the accident. Mark and my life under the microscope. I need to take things at my own pace. I can't just jump back into the public eye like nothing happened."

There's a moment of silence on the other end of the line. "Fine. Just think about it, okay? And hey, I hate to bring it up, but you've also got a contract to consider."

I hang up the phone and sigh in frustration. I know Mike means well. I'm just not ready.

Is that really true?

Lately things seem brighter. Being here, surrounded by nature and away from the hustle and bustle, it's healing. I was holed up alone in my house for so long, and now I'm venturing out again. And then there's Felix. Just thinking about his smile makes my heart skip a beat. His warmth and energy make me feel alive again. Makes me feel things I haven't let myself feel since Mark. The feelings terrify me, but maybe it's time to confront my past and embrace the future again.

A KNOCK AT THE door startles me from my writing. I glance at the clock and see it's early afternoon. *Where has the time gone?* I smile at the knowledge I've lost hours working on *Peril in the Mountains.*

My grin widens when I open the door to find Felix standing on the porch.

"Hey," he says cheerfully. "I hope I'm not disturbing you, but it's such a beautiful afternoon, I thought you might like to join me for a hike up to Sweetwater Falls."

"A hike?"

He chuckles. "It's not too strenuous, I promise." He holds up a backpack. "I've even packed a picnic, in case you needed more tempting. What'd you say?"

His enthusiasm is infectious. I contemplate my manuscript for a moment, but who am I kidding? I'm not saying no to an afternoon spent with Felix. "That sounds great. Give me a couple of minutes to get changed."

I throw on a change of clothes and pad in socked feet back to the living room. I watch Felix from the corner of my eye as I lace up my hiking boots. He's practically bouncing with excitement. I stifle a laugh. *Oh, to be that young and enthusiastic again.*

As we head out into the brisk afternoon, I zip up my jacket. Felix chatters away as we head up the mountain, pointing out various plants along the well-worn path. It's obvious he's in his element out here, surrounded by nature and the familiar environment where he grew up. The hike is a reminder that there's so many beautiful things to experience in the world.

The trail winds higher into the mountains, the valley stretching out below. We've only been hiking for three quarters of an hour, but it feels as if we're a million miles from anywhere, and my troubles seem so far away. We walk in comfortable silence for a while longer until we round a bend in the path and suddenly the falls come into view. It's spectacular. Water cascades down the rock face, the sound echoing around us.

Felix grins at my reaction. "It's something, isn't it?"

I nod. "I can't believe the cabins are so close to something like this. I can see why you loved running wild as a kid."

We settle on a flat rock overlooking the falls. I grab the blanket I shoved in my pack and a couple of bottles of water while Felix unpacks a simple picnic of cookies, apples, and a thermos of hot chocolate.

As we eat, Felix tells me more about the area. His voice is soothing as he tells tales of his adventures up here. I feel lighter and lighter as I breathe in the mountain air and enjoy the inspiring view.

"Mark would have loved this," I murmur.

"What was that?"

It's only when Felix asks the question that I realize I said the words out loud. I could brush it away but decide to answer. Perhaps talking about Mark will help me move on.

"My partner," I say softly, keeping my gaze on the waterfall. "He loved the outdoors and we travelled a lot. He was a photographer and would have loved this place." My throat is thick with emotion as I continue. "He died two years ago."

"I'm sorry." Felix's voice is as soft as mine.

"I miss him every day."

Felix nods, compassion in his gaze, but doesn't say anything.

Tears prickle behind my eyes. "I don't talk about Mark much. It's been a rough couple of years and I sort of lost myself for a while there. I guess I've been hiding away from the world." I wipe my eyes with the back of my hand and sit up straighter. "Sorry, I'm being such a downer. It really is time I put it behind me."

Felix places a hand on my thigh. "Hey, you'll move on when you're ready."

I huff a laugh. "If only my agent agreed with you."

"Agent?"

I nod. "Mike thinks enough time has passed and I should get back on the marketing trail. Book signings, conferences, interviews... all things to put me back in the public eye and ensure I hit the bestseller lists again. Maybe an Agatha Award."

"Wow." Felix's eyes are wide as he studies me.

Shit! I've let the cat out of the bag. "Yeah, um... I've got one or two of those under my belt."

"No, I don't mean *wow* about any awards. I mean *wow* that he thinks you can turn off your emotions on schedule." His hand rubs a small circle on my thigh.

I meet his eyes, floored by the understanding I see there. I nod and place a hand over his.

"I'm sorry I didn't tell you sooner. I came here to get away from all that—the expectations, the pressure to produce another bestseller. After Mark died, I just couldn't do it anymore. I needed an escape."

"I'd like to hear more about him."

"Yeah?"

Felix's expression relaxes. "Sure. You said you'd been travelling?" He grabs the thermos and pours hot chocolate into chipped enamel mugs.

I take the mug and wrap my hand around its warmth. Soon I'm sharing tales of a trip to Bali and adventures to see some temples.

"It sounds amazing," Felix says.

"I've never seen Mark move so fast, but the monkeys ran off with the lens cap, cheeky little shits," I finish.

Felix's laughter is light and bright, and I join in. It's good to reminisce without the familiar ache of loneliness.

We finish the hot chocolate sharing vacation stories until Felix reaches over and squeezes my hand. "Come on. It's getting cold and we've got nearly an hour's walk back."

We pack up the remnants of the picnic and head back onto the trail. The thought of spending another hour in Felix's company puts a spring in my step, but all too soon, we're back at my cabin.

We look at each other as we stand on the porch. The moment is heavy with possibility. My heart pounds as I turn to Felix. "Thank you for today. For... everything." I have no idea how to put my thoughts into words. I feel like I've turned some sort of corner.

Felix's eyes sparkle as he smiles. "I had an amazing after-noon. Perhaps we can get together again soon?"

I want to—so much. He's younger than me, but we have a connection and I can't deny the powerful attraction. Before I can overthink it, I take his hand in mine. It's not a friendly handshake, I'm clasping his hand because I want—no, I *need* the connection. "I'd really like that," I say.

His grin tells me everything I need to know. He squeezes my hand, his thumb tracing small circles over my skin, sending a shiver through me. Slowly, he reaches up and brushes a lock of hair back from my forehead. His fingers trail down the side of my face in a feather-light caress that makes my breath hitch.

"Kit," he murmurs, his voice a whisper. "Can I?"

My heart pounds in anticipation. I give the slightest nod. He leans in, closing the distance between us. His lips meet mine, soft and tentative at first. My eyes drift shut as I return the kiss, reveling in the sweet sensation. We break apart, foreheads touching, as my pulse races.

I want nothing more than to pull Felix into my arms, but he steps back. His smile is gentle, his words whispered. "See you soon, Kit."

He backs away with a smile, then turns and takes the porch steps two at a time. I watch him cross the yard. He doesn't turn around but lifts a hand into the air as if he knows I'm still watching.

I grin as I go inside. For the first time in a long while, I'm looking forward to what tomorrow brings.

Chapter Twelve

Felix

The last week has been the best I can remember for a long time. I laugh to myself—I've been getting up at the crack of dawn and working my ass off, but I've spent the evenings with Kit and they've been the highlight of my day. Who'd have thought I'd get so much enjoyment from simply watching a movie, or playing a game of Monopoly? The only disappointment is there have been no repeats of the kiss we shared. But I promised myself I'd take it slowly, let Kit lead the way. He's like a skittish colt I don't want to scare away.

Today's shift was brutal. Every person in Collier's Creek seemed in need of coffee and I'm exhausted from hours spent behind the espresso machine. Will deserved time off to spend with his son, but next time I'm getting one of the part-timers to pick up his shift. My feet ache as I make the way around the cabin, picking up clothes from the floor of the bedroom, and heading to the washer. I flick on the light because it's gotten so dark—weird because it's only four in the afternoon. I shove the clothes into the machine and add some Tide just as the rain starts. *Damn!* I was going to give Uncle Shawn a hand fixing the gate, but from the ferocity of the drops on the tin roof, that won't be happening. Not unless I want to get drenched.

The storm is out of the blue. Rain pounds against the windows and the wind howls around the cabin. I look outside; there's no sign of the storm abating—the sky is black with ominous clouds. I fire off a text to Uncle Shawn, checking in that he's okay. Once I get his reply, I pocket my phone and head back to the window.

The branches of the trees whip in the wind and Kit's cabin is barely visible through the driving rain. A light glows in the distance, evidence he's home, but I knew that already because I'd scoped out his Jeep when I'd arrived home half an hour ago.

Suddenly there's an almighty crash as a massive branch falls from the tall pine tree nearest Kit's cabin. The noise drowns out the rain and my throat tightens at the sight. *Fuck!*

I don't stop to think. I rip my jacket from the hook by the door, grateful I'm still wearing my boots, and head out into the storm. Icy rain lashes against my face, stinging like needles on my skin. My heart pounds as I splash through pools of water. I can hardly see, but I don't slow down. By the time I reach his cabin, I'm soaked to the bone.

My heart slows a little as I draw close. The branch hasn't landed directly on top of the cabin as I feared, but rests against the side wall in a tangle of smaller branches. I take the porch steps two at a time and pound on his door.

"Kit!"

I hammer on the door again as I call his name, louder this time to be heard over the rain. "Kit!"

Dread knots my stomach as I decide to try the door. Before I can turn the handle, it opens and Kit's standing there, surprise written on his face.

He steps forward and I all but fall into his arms. "Thank God you're okay."

Kit hugs me back just as fiercely. "The branch fell. The window... I was trying to..." He pulls back and searches my face. "What are you doing out in this mess?"

"Fuck, Kit. I was so damn scared when I saw the branch fall. I had to make sure you were safe."

Kit pulls me into another bone-crushing hug as the storm rages around us. I soak up his warmth for a minute, relieved that he's okay, before pulling away. "I should check the damage."

Kit nods. "The window in the bedroom is broken. The branch is coming through the opening."

"Okay, let me check it out."

Kit grabs his coat from the hook by the door and steps onto the porch.

"Wait here," I say. "No point both of us getting soaked. I'll let you know what I find."

I pull my collar up and step back into the downpour. Rounding the cabin, I look up at the tree. *Damn, it could have been a hell of a lot worse.* As it is, a huge branch has broken through the window. I manage to pull it enough to free it from the opening, although it still rests against the cabin. The rain continues, a little softer now, but it's freezing out here.

I return to the porch where Kit waits, concern on his face.

"I've cleared it from the window."

"Thank God," he says. "We should board up the window, though."

"Yeah. We can nail a tarpaulin over the frame. I've got one I use for camping. I'll go grab it and some tools from the cabin." I leave Kit huddled under the porch roof and dash back out into the rain, but it only takes me a few minutes to return with supplies.

"You get everything you need?" Kit asks, taking the toolbox from me.

I nod before realizing I won't be able to reach the top of the window from the ground. "Fuck! I don't have a ladder."

"It's okay, we can cover it up from the inside," Kit says, already entering the cabin. "Follow me."

"Coming." I toe off my boots on the porch and shrug off my coat before entering the cabin. My socked feet squelch on the boards as I follow Kit to the bedroom. It's freezing as the wind howls through the broken window, driving rain into the room.

"Shit!" Kit holds out an arm to halt my progress. "Stop."

"What is it?"

"There's glass all over the floor. Give me a sec and I'll grab the broom."

He sweeps the floor while I sort through the toolbox, grabbing a hammer and some nails. Once the glass is clear, we work together to cover the opening. Kit holds the tarpaulin in place while I hammer nails to secure it. The wind makes it an awkward task and my frozen fingers mean the job takes double the time, but eventually the window's covered. I sag in relief.

"It's not going to do much to keep out the cold, and I'm sure some water will still get in, but at least it will minimize damage to the bedroom," Kit says.

"I couldn't care less about the cabin." I step forward and grasp his upper arms. "I'm just glad you weren't injured." My heart is still beating a mile a minute, imagining what could have happened if the tree had crashed onto the roof of the cabin.

Kit meets my gaze and I'm sure he can see the emotions as they flicker across my face. I care about him. He's important to me. His face softens as he touches my cheek, his palm warm against my cold skin.

"You're going to catch your death of cold. You should get out of these wet clothes," he finally murmurs. "I'll get you a towel."

I nod, unable to speak, struck by his concern, but follow him to the bathroom. My fingers don't co-operate and I fumble with my sodden clothing. He ends up helping me out of my sweater and socks.

"Have a warm shower. I'll stoke the fire and make us a hot drink," he says as he straightens, then leaves me alone to dry off.

I peel off the rest of my clothes, aware of his presence just beyond the wall. My skin tingles, and not just from the cold. I use the time under the warm water to get myself under control. Thunder booms in the distance, shaking the small cabin. The rain continues to pelt down, but now the adrenalin surging through my body is for an entirely different reason.

When I emerge in a towel, Kit's stoking the fireplace. I clear my throat. "Do you, uh, have anything I can borrow?"

He turns and for a moment just looks at me, eyes traveling down my body and back up again. Heat rises in his gaze. I swallow hard, pulse racing. Then he shakes himself and hurries to the bedroom. He returns with a handful of clothes. "Here, these should fit."

He holds them out, but instead of taking the bundle, I grab his wrist before he can pull his hand back. His eyes widen, and his nostrils flare. I hear the sharp intake of his breath. But I don't let go. I'm not sure what's come over me and suddenly I'm unsure. Nervous. But I needn't be.

Kit steps closer. The fingers of his free hand trace the lines of my chest, dipping into the hollow above my sternum before stroking over muscle. My breath hitches as he grazes my nipple, sending a jolt of electricity to my groin. My knees weaken when he leans forward and presses a kiss above my heart.

"You're beautiful," he whispers.

I don't think I've ever felt as cherished as I do in that moment.

I let go of his wrist but only because I need more of him. The pile of clothes land at our feet. I reach out and tug at Kit's shirt, pulling it from his waistband so I can slide my hands over his flesh. I love that he shudders at the first touch.

I tilt my face upwards and Kit's lips descend onto mine. This kiss isn't tentative—there's no repeat of our first two gentle kisses. This kiss is all open mouths and exploring tongues. It's a kiss that's the result of weeks of lustful yearning.

We break apart, but only so I can slide Kit's shirt up and over his head. I groan as I expose his broad chest with its generous smattering of chest hair. He's built so differently to me, and I love the contrast. My smooth skin. His rugged chest. My fairness to his dark. But most of all, I love the fire I see reflected at me from those amazing eyes of his.

I move to the buttons of his jeans, popping them open. He toes off his shoes and together we rid him of his jeans. There's an urgency burning like a fire inside me.

Kit's fingers curl into my hair, tugging me up into another searing kiss. I push his boxers down, breaking the kiss just long enough to get rid of my towel, until we are standing there, hard and aching. The air leaves my lungs in a whoosh when Kit pulls me to him, and I arch into his touch. It's clear he wants me as much as I want him.

He breaks the kiss again, tugging me to the rug in front of the fireplace, where we tumble to the floor in a pile of tangled limbs.

Chapter Thirteen

Kit

Blood pounds through my veins as I lie on the rug with Felix on top of me. His hands grasp my biceps as he kisses me. There's no space between us, his strong body hard against mine. I groan as he grinds against me, kissing me harder. Heat pools in my belly and my cock throbs with need.

His kiss is desperate and when he finally pulls his mouth from mine, I drag in a gulp of much needed air. Felix looks down at me with glazed eyes, his mouth swollen and glistening. He looks as shell-shocked as I feel. *Holy shit.*

I reach up and pull his face toward me, taking his lips again. He opens to me, his tongue hot and wet as our breaths mingle. I run my hands over his body as I swallow the sexy sounds he's making—quiet moans and sexy grunts. The skin beneath my palms is soft and warm, but the muscles of his back are hard and unyielding. His ass is rounded and as I cup his cheeks, he flexes, pushing into me. I groan as his cock pushes against mine.

Needing more friction, I hold him close and undulate my hips. He gasps and buries his face against my throat, breathing against me in hot pants, his hips echoing my movements. We rub against each other, my cock hard as steel, desire building in my belly.

Oh my God.

I could come like this—between the friction and the sounds Felix is making, I'm on fire. But I want to take my time, to enjoy this moment. I want to see his face as he takes his pleasure. I want to *give* him his pleasure.

Before I think any more about it, I wrap an arm around his middle and flip us over. Felix lands on his back with a surprised grunt, panting and dazed. He smiles and wraps his arms around my neck as I lower my head to kiss him breathless again, then squirms as I kiss my way across his jaw and down his neck. He grips my head as I trail my tongue across his clavicle and make my way down his chest. He swears when I lick the dusky bud of his nipple and shouts when I pull it into my mouth.

"Fucking hell." Felix arches off the floor, clawing at my biceps as I nip and suck. His whole body is shaking with need. "Kit, please."

I lift to my elbows to study his face. Firelight plays on his skin and the brown of his eyes is eclipsed by black. He reaches for me, pulling me down into another of those spectacular kisses. Then he slips a hand between us and wraps it around my cock. *Fuck!*

I groan at the contact, surprised I don't explode then and there. His hand is hot and his grip firm, and I'm rock hard as I push through his fist. Raising on one arm, I fumble between us, knocking his hand out of the way, and wrapping my bigger hand around us both. I draw my hand up and down, watching his reactions, finding out what he likes.

"Oh, fuck yeah," he groans. "Fuck, so good."

The hard silken length of his cock moves against mine, and orgasm threatens. There's no way I want this over soon, so I put all my focus on Felix. He pushes into the tunnel of my hand, undulating as he fucks my fist. From the way he's trembling, I can tell he's close and I want nothing more than to bring him to climax. But Felix has other ideas because the next moment he's pushing up and scrambling from beneath me. He pushes the coffee table out of the way, giving us more room, then shoves me back down onto my back. He doesn't muck around, diving straight down and taking my cock into his mouth.

Fuck! I instinctively arch from the floor, forcing myself deeper, but he takes it all. He encourages me to the back of his throat, setting up a fast and strong rhythm that drives me out of my mind. I grab handfuls of rug to stop myself from grabbing his head. I let him set the pace and give myself over to the glorious blowjob. Raising my head, I follow his every movement. It's hard to hold myself together at the sight of his lips wrapped around my cock as I thrust in and out, and a minute or so later, it's all over as I explode into his mouth. He takes everything I give him and sucks me dry. When things become too sensitive, I haul him up my body.

He holds himself up on his arms and looks down at me. His lips are swollen and glistening and when we kiss, his mouth tastes of me, salty and slightly bitter. His cock presses into my belly as we continue to kiss. I reach for him. He's wet at the tip, and I use my thumb to spread the moisture around the head of his cock. He shudders at the touch, so I do it again before stroking along his length. "You feel so good, Felix."

"So do you," he says, his voice breathy. He's impossibly hard as he starts to fuck my fist. "Don't... don't... stop."

I can hear the strain as his body vibrates and love seeing him on the edge and knowing I'm the one to put him there. I speed up my movements, pumping his cock until I feel him stiffen. He throws his head back and groans as heat floods between us.

Jesus. So fucking hot!

I gentle my touch and work him through his climax, never taking my eyes from him. I don't want to miss a moment of the pleasure I can see in his expression.

Finally he slumps, a satisfied smile on his flushed face. "Oh my God, Kit."

"Yeah, oh my God."

I LIE AWAKE LONG after we've cleaned up and Felix has drifted off to sleep in my arms. The storm still rages outside, but the turmoil in my heart is pleasantly absent.

Firelight casts a warm glow over Felix's sleeping face. He looks young like this, vulnerable in a way that makes my chest ache. I brush a stray lock of blond hair off his forehead, struck by how much he's come to mean to me just a few weeks. It's fucking scary, but there's not a lot I can do about it. I stroke his bare arm, listening to his soft snores and the rain on the roof.

He stirs in his sleep, murmuring something unintelligible. I shush him with a soft kiss to his forehead. He curls against me and I pull the blanket up over his shoulder. "It's alright," I whisper. "I've got you."

My eyes close as I drift to sleep to the steady rise and fall of Felix's chest against mine.

I wake slowly, blinking my eyes open to find sunlight streaming through the cabin window. I turn my head and take in the fireplace that has burned down to embers, disoriented for a moment at finding myself on the rug on the floor. Then I take in the warm body pressed against my back and memory comes flooding back. The storm, the tree branch crashing through the bedroom window, Felix's frantic dash through the driving rain to secure the cabin—his desperation to make sure I was okay. And then afterwards. Heat pools low in my belly at the thought of last night, and I smile, pulling him closer.

He stirs, mumbling something as he wakes. I prepare myself for awkwardness, but Felix simply turns in my arms and presses a kiss to the side of my neck. "Morning."

I can't resist and nuzzle his hair. He smells clean, scented vaguely of my soap, but also of his own scent with a hint of sex underneath. He snuggles closer to my chest, one of his legs threading through mine. "How did you sleep?" I ask.

He pulls away to meet my gaze. His eyes are soft with sleep and he smiles in a way that makes my heart skip a beat. "The best sleep I've had in ages."

"Playing hero must have worn you out," I joke.

He waggles his brows. "Something sure wore me out. Did *you* sleep okay?" His fingers graze my arm as he speaks.

"I did. Although this old body isn't used to the hard floor."

He chuckles, his hand moving to my caress my chest. "There's nothing old about this body, as you proved last night."

I'm sure I blush. "How about I get you some breakfast? I'm a whiz at French toast."

"Is that so? And here I thought you might want to stay here with me a little longer." His hand slides down my side, making his intentions clear.

He tilts his face and I kiss him, slow and sweet. It's the perfect way to start the day.

CHAPTER FOURTEEN

Kit

Collier's Creek is different at night. Streetlamps softly light the pavement and quiet descends on the town. Only one or two vehicles travel down Main Street. Most of the stores are closed. We stop outside Ellis Books. Light from within illuminates the entrance and through the front windows, I can see the people inside. I'm overcome with nerves at the idea of an evening spent socializing—it's been so damn long since I've attended an event.

"Ready to have some fun?" Felix asks. He looks amazing tonight in black jeans and a knitted sweater by some designer they used to stock at the retail store where he worked.

My heart races, caught between excitement at the idea of being with Felix and apprehension. I force a smile. "Of course."

Felix gives my hand a reassuring squeeze. "It's not too late. We don't have to go if you'd rather give it a miss. Although I've got to say, Logan's wine and cheese nights are a lot of fun. I've been told he's done Romance and Rose, and Mystery and Merlot so far."

I squeeze Felix's hand in return. We've been spending a lot of time together at the cabins and he deserves a night out, plus I know he wants me to experience more of the town instead of hiding myself away. "Let's do this."

Logan greets us as we enter. "Kit, Felix! So glad you could make it!"

"Wouldn't miss it for the world," Felix replies, his usual effervescent self, giving Logan a quick hug.

Logan leads us inside. "Hang up your coats and come on through. Let's get you both a drink."

It seems half the town has turned up, laughter and conversation filling the room. The sweet spiced aroma of mulled wine fills the air and soon we're holding glass mugs of the ruby red liquid. I take a sip, allowing the warmth to spread through my chest. Hopefully a glass or two of wine will help me relax.

"Thanks for inviting me, Logan," I say. "It looks like it's the place to be."

He chuckles. "I'd like to say folks are here purely for the books, but there aren't many events on the Collier's Creek calendar at the moment."

"This is delicious." I indicate the mulled wine.

"Isn't it?" He grins. "It's Gramps Ellis' special recipe."

"Speaking of Gramps," Felix says, glancing around the room, "I should go say hi to him. I haven't seen him since I've returned to town." He gives my arm a gentle squeeze. "I'll be right back."

I watch as he crosses the room to join a group of people. I take another sip of my wine and as I stand here, watching him with his friends, I realize I'm happy.

When I look back to Logan, he's got one eyebrow in the air. It occurs to me my feelings for Felix are probably written all over my face, however, he doesn't call me on it. Instead, he points to the cheeseboard on the counter. "Try some cheese. It's the best Wyoming has to offer. There's an amazing cave-aged sheep's milk, and a smoked Gouda that's to die for."

"Sure." I take a cracker with a wedge of cheese.

"Excuse me for a moment," Logan says. "I've got some more guests to welcome."

He heads off, leaving me with my wine and cheese. The bookstore is full of people, everyone having a great time by all appearances. My gaze falls on Felix across the room where he's standing with an older man, Mrs. Hendricks, Georgia, and another young woman, all of them laughing at something. Suddenly he looks across the room and his eyes meet mine. His smile widens, lighting up his face, and drawing me like a beacon.

"Hey, Kit!" Georgia leans in to kiss my cheek when I approach. "Come join us! I know you know Mrs. Hendricks. And this is my friend, Penny," she says, tossing an arm around the shoulders of the woman next to her. "And have you met Mr. Ellis?"

I nod to Mrs. Hendricks and Penny, then hold my hand out to Mr. Ellis. "Kit Winters. It's nice to meet you."

The old man has a surprisingly strong handshake. "Call me Larry, or Gramps. Everyone else does."

"In honor of Halloween just passing, the theme of the night is horror," Felix says. "We were discussing our favorite horror movies." He loops an arm around my waist. The warmth of his touch seeps through my shirt and feels possessive, something I find I like.

Mrs. Hendricks throws me a strange look. I can't read her expression.

"You were talking about *Psycho*, Mrs. Hendricks," Georgia prompts, drawing her attention away.

"Oh, yes," she finally says, "I was just saying how much I enjoyed it."

"Really?" I ask. I wouldn't have pegged her for a horror fan. "What drew you to that movie?"

"It's classic Hitchcock," she replies. "So much tension. I just love the suspense."

I listen as they share stories of the movies that have left them terrified. I'm not a fan of horror movies, but it's nice to be part of the conversation. I turn to Gramps. "Do you have a favorite horror movie?"

He shakes his head. "I prefer to read, but there are some classic books that have been adapted for film. We have a wonderful selection of horror books here in the store. I chose some of my favorites for tonight." He points to a table where some books are on display.

"Gramps owns the store," Felix says.

"Been working here since I was a kid," Gramps adds. "But times are changing. There was no wine with books back in my day, just books."

"I need little more than a good book," Penny says.

Georgia laughs. "But everything's better with wine."

"Speaking of wine," Felix says, "I'm going to get another mug. Anyone else?"

Georgia, Penny, and I trail Felix to the refreshment table, where he ladles out the wine. The aroma of cinnamon and clove scents the air. The entire atmosphere of the bookstore, with its low lighting and soft music, is warm and inviting. But it's the look on Felix's face that gives me the most plea-sure—it's clear he's enjoying himself.

He puts down the ladle and turns to me. "Have you read much horror?" he asks.

"Not really." I shrug. "A few Stephen King novels. I'm not usually a horror fan, but I enjoyed them. He sure is the master of the genre."

"He's outstanding, isn't he?" Penny agrees.

"Let's go check out the books on display," Georgia says, hooking her arm through my elbow. I find myself drawn along beside her, glancing at Felix over my shoulder. He smirks, making me wonder if I'm about to endure a third degree.

The books chosen by Gramps are an eclectic mix of horror novels from the classics through to the current new releases. As other people approach the display, I end up chatting about novels with strangers and it's comfortingly familiar. It's fascinating to listen to differing opinions and hear their recommendations, and I'm surprisingly happy to be immersed back in the world of books and reading after being away for so long.

I eventually wander back to the refreshment table and grab a bottle of water, thankful to avoid Georgia's inquisition. The room is buzzing with people enjoying themselves, chatting, laughing, and indulging in refreshments. It's more like a party in someone's home with close friends, not a business event, but I'm pleased to see Logan ringing up a few sales. His efforts at hosting the event are paying off.

Felix is across the room, but he comes and joins me. "Sorry about Georgia," he says. "I would have come and rescued you, but you looked like you were having fun. Are you enjoying yourself?" he asks.

I smile. "You know what? I am. It's not what I expected."

Logan appears at our side. "What did you expect?"

"I'm used to more formal events, with a big push for book sales. This is more relaxed. You've done an outstanding job, Logan."

"You go to a lot of book events?" Logan asks.

I freeze for a moment. I look to Felix, who smiles in encouragement. *Got to take that first step sometime*, I think to myself. *Can't hide away forever.*

"Not lately." I take a sip of water, my throat suddenly dry. "But I have in the past. I've published a few books and had to hit the publicity trail with each release."

"Really?" Logan's clearly intrigued, his brows raised.

"Remember the series we spoke about that first day I came into the store?"

He frowns as he thinks for a moment. "The *Mountain Mystery Files*? Wait! You're Christopher Winters?"

I chuckle, but butterflies are dancing in my stomach as I leave my safe space of anonymity. "That'd be me."

"Holy shit!"

Logan's loud exclamation draws the attention of others in the room. "What's going on?"

I look around the now familiar faces and take a deep breath. "I was just telling Logan that I've published some cozy mystery books."

I can see the curiosity in their eyes. Felix's hand lands on my lower back, his presence a steady anchor.

"The *Mountain Mystery Files*," Logan repeats.

"I also write a little romance, under a different pseudonym."

"You mentioned that the other day," Logan says, "but I had no idea." His gaze falls on Mrs. Hendricks. "Well, I had some idea."

Mrs. Hendricks smirks. "I did a little sleuthing of my own. I thought you looked familiar, although you had more of a beard then. I saw you once being interviewed on a morning show, but for the life of me, I couldn't remember your name." She taps her temple. "This old noggin' isn't as good as it used to be, but I told Logan that you were an author. "

"But I hadn't put two and two together until now," Logan says.

"I think it's amazing," Georgia says. "A celebrity in our midst—"

"I wouldn't go that far," I say, waving her off.

"Would you sign a book for me?" a lady asks.

"Oh, yes. Me too." A number of people seem keen, and the mood changes as they focus their attention on me.

My stomach tightens, but Felix steps in. "Not now. This is meant to be a fun night out for Kit, not work."

"Exactly," Logan agrees. "Now, who wants some more mulled wine? Plus, we got a new shipment of *How to Sell A Haunted House* today for those of you who've been waiting."

Logan winks as walks away. I'm surprised by how easily the conversation resumes and I'm no longer the center of attention.

Felix steps closer, wrapping his arm around my waist and I lean into him, appreciating the support. As we stand there, I notice an older woman with pinkish hair watching us from across the room. Her frown doesn't escape my attention, but I push away any negative thoughts. Tonight is about having a good time, and I won't let anyone's judgment dampen my spirits.

"Let's get some more wine," Felix suggests, releasing me from his hold and grabbing my hand. "You deserve a toast to celebrate coming out."

I huff a laugh. Sure, I've come out as an author to the good folk of Collier's Creek, but it also feels as if I've taken a step forward with Felix by bringing our relationship into the open. Although I'm not exactly sure what the status of our relationship is.

We raise our filled mugs.

"Cheers." Felix taps my mug. "You've come a long way since you first arrived here."

He's right. My life has changed so much since coming to Collier's Creek. It may only be baby steps, but I can feel the loneliness that has weighed me down for so long is being replaced by a sense of belonging.

Chapter Fifteen

Felix

"Hey, Felix," Will says, popping his head into the kitchen where I'm doing a load of dishes. "I was wondering if it'd be okay if I came in late tomorrow. I need to attend something at the school."

"Of course. No problem," I say, loading another plate into the dishwasher.

"Thanks, man."

I grab a tea towel and dry my hands as I head toward him. "How's Mav doing at school?"

"Good. Great actually." He grins, like he always does when talking about his son.

"He's a cool kid."

Will nods. "The best. Do you see yourself having kids one day?"

The question takes me back. *Kids?* It's not something I've thought much about, but yeah, I could see myself with an ankle-biter or two. *Especially if Kit was in the picture*, a little voice whispers in my head.

"One day. Not sure if I'm ready for the responsibility yet. Still got my wild oats to sow, you know?"

Will throws back his head in laughter. "Yeah, I get it. But when the time comes, just remember, it's true what they say, it takes a village. I'm just so damn lucky to have Colton and some amazing friends for support."

We head back to the front of the coffee shop, where I drop to my haunches behind the counter. It's been a busy morning and I need to refill the paper roll in the register ready for the lunch rush. I grab the box of rolls when Will taps my head.

"Psst. Gorgeous broody man alert."

My mood lifts instantaneously, and a smile lifts my lips. I rise to my feet as Kit approaches the counter.

"I've got to do... that thing. You know, out the back." Will disappears into the kitchen leaving me with Kit.

"Morning, stranger," I say. "Welcome to Coffee and Cuddles."

"Cuddles, huh?" Kit's got a smile a mile wide.

"Only for very special customers."

His brows raise. "And what exactly does one need to do to get one of these cuddles?"

I lean over the counter, crooking a finger to encourage him closer.

"How about a repeat of last night?" I whisper.

Kit's laughter is like a reward. I love to see him smiling instead of scowling, something he does more and more lately.

"Are we still on for tonight?" I ask, moving to make Kit's usual espresso.

"Absolutely. I thought we could watch a movie," Kit says. "Or we could go out for a meal if you'd prefer. You mentioned something about Fox's?"

"Nah. We'll save that for another night. A movie sounds perfect." I can't think of a better way to spend an evening than curled up in front of the fire with my head in Kit's lap while we watch something on the TV. I've become a homebody, just enjoying his company as we get to know each other. I hand him his coffee. "I'll bring over something for dinner."

Kit pops a note into the tip jar. "Not wanting to brave my cooking?" he asks. Kit's proven once or twice over the past couple of weeks that his cooking skills are limited. Very limited.

"Ahh…"

"How about we cook together? You can give me another lesson."

"Hmm." I tap my chin and pretend to give it serious consideration. "You know what they say about old dogs."

"Hey!" He leans over the counter and grasps my arm. His thumb strokes slowly up and down the pulse point of my wrist. He drops his voice. "I'm sure I can teach you a new trick or two."

My face heats along with the rest of my body. I can't wait for tonight to arrive and groan at the thought I have to get through hours and hours of work until we can be alone. "See you later," I manage to squeak out.

He arches his brow. "I'll look forward to it."

I follow his exit, noting Mrs. Hendricks standing nearby. She obviously been observing our interaction.

"What can I get for you, Mrs. Hendricks?" I ask as she steps up to the counter.

"Six of your delicious scones, thank you, Felix. Some of the blueberry ones, and some chocolate chip."

"Sure thing." I unfold a cardboard box and pick up the tongs.

She sets her purse on the counter. "I've noticed how close you've become with Kit lately."

I pause what I'm doing and glance at her. She's rummaging around for something in the depths of her purse. "H-hmm." I say non-committal.

"He's a very nice man." She's feigning casual, but I can see her mind at work. "I can see why you'd find him attractive."

"Kit and I are… getting to know each other." *Not that it's any of your business.*

"You know, after the evening at the bookstore, I looked up his biography online. He's a very well-respected author and has sold a lot of books."

"Yes," I say, selecting a scone and placing it in the box. "He's even won some awards for his writing."

"There were online articles. Did you know he had a partner for many years and that his partner died?"

I grit my teeth. "I did know. Mark died a couple of years ago. It was very tragic."

"By all accounts, he's been a recluse ever since. He hasn't released a new book in a long time and people are complaining about the delay."

The tongs clatter to the counter and I snap the lid of the box closed. "I'm not sure what your point is, Mrs. Hendricks."

She gives up on whatever it was she was searching for in her purse and meets my gaze. I'm sure she can tell I'm not happy. "I just want to make sure you know what you're getting yourself into, dear."

"I appreciate your concern, but I don't think we should talk about him behind his back. He likes his privacy."

She leans across and pats my hand. "Of course. It's just that he's been through a lot. He comes with baggage and I know you've had your own problems recently—"

"Kit's past is his own business," I say firmly. "As is mine."

"Alright, dear. I'm just looking out for you now your mother isn't around." She delves back into her purse and pulls out some notes. "How is Susan, by the way? Still enjoying Florida?"

She's been a friend of my parents since before I was born and I know she's just looking out for my well-being, so I bite back what I really want to say. I ring up her purchase while giving her an update on Mom and Dad.

Unfortunately her words continue swirling in my thoughts and dull the brightness of my afternoon.

As soon as the coffee shop is closed for the day, I hightail it over to the general store.

Georgia is at the shelves of cereal restocking Cheerios. Her face lights up when she sees me.

"Hey, hon. I didn't expect to see you this afternoon. No hot date planned with your man?"

"He's not my man." The words leave my mouth unbidden. They also feel like a lie. "And I wish everyone would stop being so interested in my love life."

"Oh!" She places her hand on her hips. "Where's my happy Felix disappeared to and who is this stranger in his place?"

I sigh. "Sorry, Georgia, I didn't mean to snap."

She steps closer and puts a hand on my arm. "What's wrong, honey?"

I look around the store. There's someone on the far side, but no one close enough to overhear our conversation. The last thing I want is more gossip. I lower my voice anyway. "Mrs. Hendricks stopped by earlier. She said some stuff about Kit and his past. Stuff she found online."

"You know her, Felix. She likes to be in everyone's business. And Kit's a bit of a celebrity, so it's not surprising she looked him up. I'm sure half the town will be doing their own research. You know how it is."

"I know. It's just she said some stuff."

"What kind of stuff?" she asks, eyes filled with concern.

I don't want to recount the details of Kit's past, although I'm sure Georgia will find out anyway if she doesn't know already. "The point she was making is that I should be careful. He's got a history—"

"You knew that, and we all have a history, hon."

"It's a lot to take on." I hate that Mrs. Hendrick's words have gotten to me, but I can help wondering if there's some truth to what she's saying.

"And you don't want to get hurt?"

That's it in a nutshell. I nod. "Am I making a mistake? I didn't expect to feel the way I do, but is it too soon? You warned me not to get into a rebound thing. What if that's what this is?"

"Look, Felix," she says gently, taking my hands in hers. "It's natural to have doubts and fears in a new relationship. But you've got to trust your own judgment and follow your heart. I know I warned you off, but I can see how good the two of you are together. You care about Kit, don't you?"

"More than anything."

"Then focus on that. Focus on how he makes you feel. You're both adults, and I'm sure you'll manage any challenges that come your way. And I'm always here for you if things don't work out. I guess what I'm saying is you don't know if you don't try."

She squeezes my hands and I feel some of the weight lifted from my shoulders.

I kiss her cheek. "You always say exactly the right thing. Plus, I'm probably over-thinking things. I don't even know how long he plans to stay in town. He could be gone tomorrow for all I know."

I don't actually think that. Kit would have mentioned it if he had any intention of leaving so soon, but he also hasn't said anything about staying long-term either. He may leave after he's written his book, and he's been making great progress lately. Suddenly, my happiness at him finding his writing groove again diminishes.

"One day a time, hon," she says.

After completing my shopping, I leave the store, but as I navigate the winding country road, I find myself deep in thought, trying to puzzle out whether Kit and I truly want the same things.

I pass by the familiar sights of Collier's Creek—the town square where Jake's Day is held each year, the quaint, old-fashioned homes, the picturesque park where families gather on weekends. It's all part of the tight-knit community I've known all my life. It must be such a different world for Kit. He's spent his entire life in the city, then spent recent years alone, nursing his grief.

Is it possible for two people from such different backgrounds to make a life together? Would he even want to? I resolve to find out.

But first to drop off Uncle Shawn's groceries. I slow down as I approach the cabins. I head through the gates and straight to Uncle Shawn's house, where I see he has a visitor. I park directly in front and get out of the car. The afternoon sun casts long shadows across the gravel road, a faint breeze rustles through the trees, carrying with it the scent of pine and earth. It's beautiful, but cold. I quickly grab the bag of groceries from the back. I smile when my gaze lands on the other bag, excited at the thought of preparing a meal with Kit.

The sound of conversation greets me as soon as I enter the house.

I stop at the kitchen doorway, hesitating when I hear Geraldine talking. She's a friend of Uncle Shawn's and a bit of a character, and she sure knows how to chat. I don't want to get pulled into a long-winded conversation, so contemplate leaving the groceries on the floor in the hall. I can always text Uncle Shawn that they're there. But what I hear next stops me in my tracks.

"… and he's so much older," Geraldine says. "I mean, what could they possibly have in common?"

"Age is just a number, Geraldine," Uncle Shawn replies. "How they feel about each other is all that matters."

Yes! Go Uncle Shawn.

"Of course, of course," Geraldine continues. "But they're bound to face some challenges. We all know how people talk in this town."

Fuck! Damn gossip! I can't believe it's the second time in one day. I know Mrs. Hendricks only has my best interest at heart, but Geraldine is just an old busy-body who likes to foist her opinions on everyone else.

"Too much, if you ask me," Uncle Shawn mutters, echoing my own thoughts. "Felix is a good kid. He has his head screwed on right. Now, let's get back to the raffle donations. That's what you came here for, right?"

"Oh, of course. The hospital fundraiser—"

"Excuse me," I interrupt, stepping into the room. "Hi, Uncle Shawn. How are you, Geraldine?" I keep my voice steady and polite as I nod her way.

Her eyes widen, her face nearly the same color as her pink-tinged hair, before she regains her composure. "I'm fine, Felix, thank you for asking. And how are you doing? Have you settled back in after your time away? I was sorry to hear about your troubles."

"Yeah, I'm good. I've got the groceries you asked me to pick up, Uncle Shawn," I say, changing the subject.

"Thank you, my boy." Uncle Shawn rises from the table and takes the bag. "Did you want to stay for supper?"

"No thanks, not tonight. I've got plans, so I'll have to take a raincheck." Geraldine opens her mouth to speak, but I don't give her time to ask any questions. "Anyway, I'll see you tomorrow to go over the project outline."

After a quick goodbye, I fly out the door. I've got a dinner to get to.

Chapter Sixteen

Kit

The phone rings just as I complete a final read through of my latest chapters. I see Mike's name on the display. It's as if the man has ESP.

I smile as I hit the answer button. "Hey, Mike, how are you?"

"Kit, you sound upbeat. I'm not interrupting, am I?"

"Actually, you've got perfect timing." I lean back in my chair, grinning at the computer screen and the document full of words. *Good* words.

"Oh! Now you've got me intrigued. The writing's still going well, I take it?"

"I've got a dozen new chapters for you." It's hard to hold back my enthusiasm. It's been a painful process to get this far, but I've turned a corner and it feels damn good.

Mike chuckles. "Well, it's about time. I haven't heard you this excited in years. Must be that small-town charm working its magic, eh?"

I smile thinking of Felix. He's been like a breath of fresh air. "I think you're going to love them, Mike. I can't wait to see what you think."

"And I can't wait to read them. Listen, now you're back on track, we should leverage what you've got going and start thinking about marketing. I know you've avoided the spotlight since... well, you know, but we've got a real chance for you to make a huge comeback."

My stomach tightens at the thought of putting myself back out there. The bookstore event went fine, but that wasn't about me. "We've already had this conversation."

"I know, but I wouldn't be doing my job if I didn't raise it again."

I sigh. The idea terrifies me, but he's right. "Let's just focus on the book for now. I'll send you the chapters tonight, and I promise I'll give some thought to promotion. Maybe we can start with some published interviews, nothing face-to-face."

"Starting slow?" Mike says. "I can work with that."

There's a knock at the door, so I cross the room, phone to my ear. "Thanks, Mike, I appreciate the support."

"I've got your back, Kit," he says. "I look forward to getting the chapters. Now get back to that manuscript."

"Slave-driver."

Mike laughs. It's nice to end the call on a positive note.

I'm still smiling when I open the door to Felix.

"Hey!" Felix says, eyes lighting up.

"Hey, you." I reach out and pull him in. He yelps with surprise, his laughter ringing out as I wrap him in a hug. He feels good in my arms, especially when he nuzzles my neck. His skin is cold, but that's not why I shiver. I close my eyes and breathe in his familiar scent. After being alone for so long, this is what I crave—Felix's presence, his touch, his smell, the way he looks at me. I allow myself another moment of indulgence before reluctantly releasing him.

"From that welcome, I'd say you're glad to see me," he says, handing over the grocery bag and taking off his coat. "You must be starving."

"I'm starving, all right, but not necessarily for whatever's in this bag."

He chuckles. "Lucky I'm here then."

"What's on the menu tonight?" I ask as I carry the groceries to the kitchen with Felix hot on my heels.

"You mean to eat, or for after?"

"I was referring to the groceries," I say as laughter bubbles out.

"Chili. Just the way my grandma made it."

I set the bag on the counter. "Mmm. And perfect on a cold night like tonight."

"Exactly what I thought. An enormous bowl of chili while sitting in front of the fire." Felix glances at the fire as he speaks. "Hey! You've created an inferno."

"I was taught by the best," I say with a wink.

He laughs and gets to unpacking the groceries.

Soon we're chopping onions and browning ground beef, and the kitchen fills with the aroma of spices. As usual, Felix supervises, instructing me in the art of making the perfect chili. Cooking together has become one of my favorite parts of our evenings.

As the chili simmers, we prepare the accompaniments and Felix keeps me laughing with funny stories from the coffee shop. By the time we sit down, my mouth's watering. I pick up my spoon and eat a mouthful.

"Mmm... you've outdone yourself again."

He grins. "I'm glad you like it, but it was a team effort."

I bark a laugh. "I don't think my stirring was much of a contribution."

"Don't sell yourself short," Felix says. "Everything tastes better when it's made with love."

My spoon stops on the way to my mouth, and I meet his eyes. *What?* I put the spoon back in the bowl and reach for my glass, my throat suddenly parched.

Felix holds my gaze for a moment before digging back into his chili. "So, how did your day go? Did you finish the chapter?"

I swallow a mouthful of wine. "I did. I finished the chapter and outlined the next. Mike called just before you arrived, and I was able to give him the good news."

"That's awesome," Felix says, his voice full of happiness. "It's really coming along now."

"Yep. I'll finish *Peril in the Mountains* before you know it." Strangely, I don't feel elation as I say the words. I should be over the moon that the book is going so well and the end is in sight, but writing that last chapter also means the end of my time in Collier's Creek. *And with Felix.* "Tell me more about the disaster at the coffee shop," I say, changing the subject back to safer ground in case I blurt out something stupid about not wanting to lose him.

Felix launches into the story he'd started earlier and I'm back on an even keel as I listen to him talk. He totally commits when telling a story, his eyes lighting up and hands gesturing wildly. It's adorable and I could listen to him all day.

After we finish our meal, I do the dishes while Felix puts away the leftovers.

"There's enough for a couple of meals," he says. "I've also put a container in the freezer. Can't have you being a starving artist."

"Thanks." I throw him a smile, warmed by the gesture. He knows I get caught up in writing and prepping meals is the last thing on my mind, just like I know he's dead on his feet from being up early at the coffee shop. But I also know he's not going to go sit down until we've cleaned up together.

We work in comfortable silence for a while, the clinking of plates and silverware punctuating the quiet. I glance at Felix standing beside me and catch him looking at me, a soft smile on his lips. My heart flutters. This moment in time is perfect, and I wish I could bottle the way I feel.

After the last dish is dry and put away, I take Felix's hand. "C'mon, let's get you off your feet." I lead him to the couch and settle him into the corner, taking off his shoes and socks before draping the blanket over his lap. I flick on the TV, setting up a movie Felix mentioned he wanted to see. By the time I've put another log on the fire, he's nearly asleep, tousled head resting on a cushion.

The couch dips as I take a seat at the other end and he stirs. I lift the edge of the blanket and pull his feet onto my lap, wrapping a hand around his slim foot. The skin is smooth under my touch as I rub his feet. He purrs like a cat, making mewling sounds as I stroke along the top of his foot.

"Oh my God, that feels so good," he murmurs.

I press a thumb into his arch. He groans in response. The sounds goes straight to my cock which I ignore. This isn't about me, this is about Felix and he's exhausted.

"Sorry, I'm such crap company," he says, as if reading my thoughts.

"Don't worry about it. You've had a long day. Besides, I'm perfectly comfortable where I am."

"Do you want to watch the movie?" he asks.

"Not unless you do."

"Put it on. You can watch while you massage my feet," he says and I can't help smiling. I hit Play but his eyelids are already drooping.

Outside, the wind whistles through the trees, but inside it's warm and peaceful. I lower the volume of the movie so it's only a soft noise in the background.

"I could stay like this forever," Felix murmurs.

"Me too," I say, meaning it completely.

His presence is a balm, and my worries seem to dissolve when he's near. I study his face lit by the glow of the fire, taking in every detail. He's so beautiful with his dark lashes fanned out above his high cheekbones. There's a faint shadow along his jaw, and a smattering of freckles across his nose. He looks so young and innocent.

He opens his eyes and catches me staring. A slow smile spreads across his face before he pulls his feet back and shuffles around on the couch. He settles back down, laying his head against my chest. The scent of his shampoo fills my nostrils, and his weight grounds me. I'm aware of him with every fiber of my being and soak up the closeness as I watch the flickering flames.

We stay curled up together for a while longer, until Felix tilts his head up. His gaze locks on mine as he raises his hand, cupping my jaw before sliding his hand behind my neck and tugging me closer. When our lips meet, it's tender and unhurried. I pour all of my feelings into the kiss, trying to convey what I'm too afraid to put into words.

I lose all track of time as we kiss, my focus narrowing to the feel of his lips, the warmth of his body against mine, how good he feels in my arms. A low heat continues to simmer in my belly, but I don't act on it.

"The movie isn't over," I mumble against his lips.

Felix huffs a soft laugh. "I don't think either one of us is paying attention."

He's right. Everything else faded away the moment his mouth found mine.

When we finally break apart, we're both breathing harder. Felix's eyes are dark, his lips kiss-swollen.

"Do you want to stay the night?" I whisper.

He nods. It's the first time he's slept over and it makes my heart sing, knowing he'll be sharing my bed all night. It doesn't take long to get ready for bed. Felix borrows a toothbrush, and I lend him a T-shirt. We climb into bed and I pull him against me.

We talk softly in the dark, and his breathing slows until he's asleep in my arms.

Chapter Seventeen

Felix

The sweet taste of maple syrup fills my mouth as I take another bite. Across from me, Kit smiles over his coffee mug, those piercing blue eyes watching my every move.

"These are amazing," I say. "You *can* cook."

He chuckles. "It's not so hard when there's a packet mix."

A faint blush colors Kit's cheeks. I've learned he's not one to accept compliments easily, but I'll keep trying.

"Seriously, these are *good*."

Okay, so maybe they're not perfect—a little misshapen and darker on the edges—but he made them specially for me. How can I not love them?

My words from last come back to me. *Everything tastes better when it's made with love.* I can't believe I said it. God, I want it to be true with every fiber of my being.

Things are fantastic between us. Being with Kit is easy. Natural, like breathing. After my disaster of a relationship with Aiden, I never imagined I could feel this way again. But Kit makes me happier than I've been in a long time. If I'm honest, happier than I've ever been.

We finish up breakfast and I clear the table, taking the dishes to the sink. Kit comes up behind me, wrapping his arms around my waist. I lean back into him, savoring his warmth.

"I wish you didn't have to go into work today," he murmurs against my neck.

"Me too, but you've got a book to finish, and I'll only get in your way." I turn and kiss him softly. "Go finish that next bestseller."

With a dramatic sigh, Kit disentangles himself, but there's a smile tugging at his lips.

"You're my inspiration, you know," he says.

I don't know what to say, but the idea of being his muse fills me with happiness, a feeling I could get used to. Instead of replying, I grab the carafe and fill a mug. "Here. I'm sure some liquid inspiration won't go astray."

Kit plants a kiss on my cheek and heads to his desk and I return to tidying the kitchen, replaying last night and our morning together. Things feel right with him. I'm letting things unfold naturally, no pressure, and with Kit by my side, I'm enjoying every moment I spend in Collier's Creek.

My phone rings just as I'm hanging up the tea towel. I grab it from the counter and see it's Uncle Shawn. I accept the call and tuck the phone under my ear as I pour myself a cup of coffee. I've got about twenty minutes until I need to leave for work.

"Hey, Uncle Shawn, what's up?" I sit on the couch and catch Kit's eye. He smiles, then opens his laptop.

"Felix, my boy! Listen, I want your opinion on somethin'. I've looked over your ideas and had a quick chat with Susan and Brian about the plans. We need to run some numbers, but we just might be able to swing it."

I can hear the excitement in Uncle Shawn's voice. I'd given him a list of ideas for building up the business, but rebranding and better marketing means modernizing the cabins, and that means money. "How can I help?"

"You're right," he says. "We seem to attract families and some older guests who've been comin' here for years. We need to attract some young-uns, you know? You've got your finger on the pulse of what's hip these days. What kind of upgrades do you think we should look at?"

I chuckle at hearing the word "hip" but it warms me to know he wants my input and is open to ideas. I don't even need to stop and think about it because the ideas have been rattling around in my head the last couple of weeks. I glance at Kit's fridge. "Well, first off, I think all three guest cabins need re-wiring. It wouldn't hurt to check the plumbing too, so we're starting with a clean slate. The cabins have rustic charm. I don't think we should lose that, but a little luxury wouldn't go astray either. The kitchens could do with new appliances and new countertops that fit the aesthetic. I don't think the cabinets need to be replaced, but new drawer and door handles would update the look. Let's see..." I tap my fingers as I mentally review my list, excited to be sharing my ideas. "New bedding, maybe new couches or at least new scatter cushions and throw rugs. Oh, and people nowadays expect good Wi-Fi and things like charging stations and Bluetooth speakers."

Uncle Shawn chuckles. "Wow, that's some list. You've got a good vision there, Felix. It won't be the same without you when you head back to the city."

My enthusiasm dims at the reminder my time here is limited.

"Maybe you'll consider staying?" he says.

"We'll see what happens," I say vaguely. "I'm really loving being back, helping at the coffee shop."

"Aww. It's great to have you around," says Uncle Shawn. "You know there's always a place for you here."

We chat a few more minutes before hanging up. I push aside the uneasiness at the thought I have to make some decisions about my life soon. For now, I'm exactly where I want to be.

LATER THAT DAY, I'M happily working away at CC's, chatting with customers and everything is running smoothly. Will's behind the espresso machine and things are quietening down after the lunch rush. As I'm clearing some empty mugs from a table, the bell above the door jingles. I look up and get the shock of my life.

"Cam!"

Cam's gaze lands on me. He crosses the room and gives me a quick hug. "Hey, Felix. It's good to see you."

"What the hell are you doing here?" I ask, clapping him on the back, then stepping back to look at him. "Checking up on me?"

"Not on your life. You've been doing an awesome job," he says, but then his smile fades.

I look at him with concern. "Is everything okay? Is Greg all right?'

"He's fine. It's Mom."

My heart sinks. "Your mom? What's wrong?"

"Her MS has relapsed. It's a pretty severe flare-up this time around."

"Oh, no. I'm so sorry, man." I know how close Cam is to his family. "What can I do?"

"There's nothing much anyone can do," Cam says. "She's got a great doctor, but only time will tell how fast and far she'll recover."

"She went into remission last time."

"Yeah, for a while. We're all holding hope that she'll respond well this time too. In the meantime, I've come back to be with the folks, drive her to appointments, help around the house, that type of stuff. I think Dad appreciates the support too."

"So you're cutting your vacation short?"

Cam huffs a laugh. "So much for the big world trip, huh? At least we got to see Australia. I'm glad we started there."

"I'm so sorry."

Cam shrugs, putting on a brave face. "It is what it is."

"So...." It hits me I could be out of a job, a job that I love. "Does that mean you'll be coming back to work?"

Cam shakes his head. "I was hoping you'd be able to keep taking care of things here a while longer."

The relief is instantaneous, and I feel like a dick. It's only his mom's illness that is stopping him from returning to work while he's in town. I give his arm a reassuring squeeze. "Of course. As long as you need."

"At least until after Christmas. Sometime in the new year."

The new year. Cam's return makes me confront the fact that this job was only ever meant to be temporary. Managing the coffee shop was a stopgap and now I need to start thinking about what I want for the future.

"Sure. I can do that." I paste on a smile. "Hey, while you're here, do you want to go over some stuff? It's easier with you being face to face."

Cam chuckles. "Time differences and doing most things via email is challenging."

We grab some coffees and move to a table in the corner. While Will takes care of the customers, Cam and I discuss an issue with suppliers and I run an idea past him. The local hospital is having a fundraiser and I want to donate some coffee cards as raffle prizes, an idea I thought of when Uncle Shawn was chatting with Geraldine. I'm happy to pay for the cards but want to put the CC's branding on them. Cam is fully on board and wants to do even more. I guess his mom's illness has provided extra incentive for him to support a great cause.

Seeing how passionate Cam is about looking out for his mom and taking some of the burden off his dad's shoulders, gets me thinking about family. Although my parents live in

Florida for most of the year, and that's where I've visited them recently, I feel like coming back to Collier's Creek is returning home. It's where I grew up, and where the family business is. Sure, the rental cabins have seen better days, but I remember when they were popular and it was a thriving business, which they can be again. The cabins are part of my roots, and coming up with ideas and discussing them with Uncle Shawn has given me a real sense of purpose.

It dawns on me that a big part of me wants to stay in Collier's Creek.

And then there's Kit. My chest warms just thinking about him. I can't believe how quickly he's made his way into my heart. We've gone from zero to full steam ahead in such a short time, but it feels *real*. I can't imagine leaving now that things are getting serious between us. However, there's no guarantee he'll stay in Collier's Creek. In fact, it's a given he'll be leaving. It's just a matter of when.

"Are you okay, dude? You spaced out for a minute there."

I shake my head and focus back on Cam. "Yeah, cool. I'd better get back to work, though, and give Will a hand. How about we get together for a drink later this week? I'd love to catch up with Greg and hear all about Australia?"

Cam pushes back from the table. "That sounds awesome. I'll call you later and we can set something up."

I give him a hug and get back to work while Cam catches up with Will. His early return has definitely given me a lot to think about.

CHAPTER EIGHTEEN

Felix

The chilly autumn air nips at my cheeks as I make my way across the town square to meet Kit. I spot him sitting on a bench, bundled up in a coat and scarf. He's scribbling in his ever-present notebook, the breeze lifting his hair. He absently pushes it back, then raises his head and looks my way, those startling blue eyes meeting mine. His face lights into a grin.

"Hey there." I plant a quick kiss to his chilled lips and hand over a hot cup of coffee. "Thought you could use something to warm you up."

"You are amazing, thanks."

"I bet you say that to all the boys," I say with a wink.

He chuckles as I take a seat beside him. "Only the amazing ones."

"So, are you ready for tonight?" I ask.

"Ready as I'll ever be."

I can't help laughing at the look on Kit's face. He's come to meet me after work as we're heading to Randy's Rodeo Grill and Bar. I'm going to give him a real taste of local town life. He looks terrified at the prospect.

I place a hand on his thigh. "You'll have a good time, I promise."

"Hmm. That remains to be seen."

"Trust me."

He turns to look at me more fully and places a hand over mine where it rests on his leg. "I do."

The words are said with such gravity, the moment heavy as something passes between us. I'm the first to look away because I want to say so much and I need to stop myself from blurting out my feelings.

Across the square, Geraldine is talking to the sheriff, JD Morgan. Her arms are flailing wildly as she gestures, her scrappy little dog barking as it pulls on its lead.

Kit takes a sip of his coffee, then gestures to them. "See that woman?" he says. "The one with the dog."

I nod. "Barkasaurus Rex."

"What?"

"The dog. Its name is Barkasaurus Rex. Geraldine is the owner."

"Right. Anyway, I overhead her talking when she walked by with another woman earlier."

"Oh God, who was she gossiping about this time?"

"Us. She was going about our age difference, and how unseemly it is."

My brows shoot up, although I guess I shouldn't be surprised given what I'd overheard when she was visiting Uncle Shawn. "I wouldn't worry too much about it. She's a notorious gossip and anything she says should be taken with a grain of salt."

Kit scowls.

"Hey, you're not taking it onboard, are you? This age gap thing?"

His jaw is tight. "It's nearly fourteen years, Felix."

"And? If we're happy, that's all the matters and what happens between us is no one else's business but ours."

Kit sighs. He squeezes my hand. "I know you're right."

"But?"

He shakes his head. "I hate people talking about me, especially when they have no idea what's really going on. After

Mark's accident, our private life was splattered all over social media."

"I'm sorry that happened to you."

"Half-truths and outright lies." Kit looks at me, sadness written in his expression. "Mark and I had argued. It was stupid, really. I was being an asshole and Mark decided to give me some space. He met his best friend for dinner to give me time to cool down, you know? Chris was driving Mark home when the car was side-swiped, and he hit a pole. Mark died instantly. Chris was in a serious but stable condition for weeks. Somehow the gossip made it to social media, and it did the rounds, at least in the literary world. Some ridiculous story about Mark having an affair."

"God, Kit. I don't know what to say. I'm sorry to have treated it as if town gossip was just a minor thing to ignore."

"I'm probably being overly sensitive."

"No, I get it. You've been through hell, and at a time when you were grieving."

Kit gives a wry chuckle. "For a while I started believing what I was reading online, even though I knew it wasn't true. And then when I heard that old biddy saying I was too old for you... well... I guess it hit home just how old I am. God, Felix, what the fuck are you doing with me?"

"Having a good time." I stand and hold out a hand. "Come on. We've got places to go and people to see."

Kit laughs, a proper laugh this time, and allows me to haul him to his feet. "I can't believe I'm letting you take me to a rodeo bar."

"I like to think you'd follow me anywhere," I say with a wink. "Now come on, cowboy."

"Yee Haw!"

WE PUSH THROUGH THE heavy doors into the lively atmosphere of Randy's. The lighting is dim, and the aroma of fried food fills the air combined with wood shavings and peanuts. I take a deep breath, savoring the familiar scent. It's been ages since I've been here and it's nice to be back. Kit glances around, taking in the rustic interior, and I try to visualize things through his eyes. The long bar, the wooden tables, the band set up at the side, and the crowded dance floor.

"Wow, Felix, this place is... incredible," Kit says, still scanning the room. He doesn't look like he wants to hightail it straight out of here, which is a win.

"Isn't it?" I reply. "There's nothing quite like a night out at Randy's."

Scanning the room, I spot Georgia at a table near the dance floor. She's in the spirit of things, her long auburn hair covered by a cowboy hat. I assume the man sitting with her is the new guy she's seeing, Trent.

"Come on." I grab Kit's hand and lead him across the room.

She sees us approach and gestures us over. "Hey, Felix! Kit! Over here!"

"Hey, Georgia!" I give her a kiss, then turn to the guy. "You must be Trent," I say, shaking his hand. "Nice to meet you, man."

"Likewise," he replies with a friendly smile.

I introduce Kit, then we settle into our seats and pour beer from the pitcher on the table.

"Kit, how's the writing going?"

"Slowly but surely," he responds, then takes a sip of beer. "How are things at the store?"

She rolls her eyes to the ceiling. "Oh my God, it's been crazy lately. It seems that vacations in mountain towns are all the rage."

"*Yellowstone* fever," I say. "Everyone's watching that show and wanting to experience ranching life."

Georgia laughs. "Maybe. Hey, Trent, what were you saying about tourism?"

Trent puts down his beer. "I work at the bank, so know a bit about local development. The new area of town is coming ahead in leaps and bounds and is really popular with tourists. Plus, there's a new resort being built about twenty miles outside of town."

"I wonder what that means for the cabin redevelopment," I muse. I'm still working on the business plan and waiting for some market research, but I know our enquiries are increasing. In fact, the only reason I haven't moved in with Uncle Shawn to free up my cabin is because of our renovation plans.

"The development in the area will flow along to local businesses," Trent says. "I don't think we have enough accommodation for the demand."

Kit nods. "What you've got is special, Felix. A resort can't match the seclusion and beauty of your location near the falls. Plus, what you want to do with the glamping is unique."

A server stops by and drops a couple of baskets of fries to the table, and another pitcher of beer.

"I hope you two have been practicing your line dancing," Georgia teases.

"Nope. But Kit has some *amazing* moves, so I'm sure he'll be fine on the dance floor." I waggle my brows.

Georgia pouts and flips me off. "I don't think we need all the details about Kit's moves."

Trent's eyes are wide and Kit chuckles at the exchange. I'm glad to see he's relaxed and at ease with the gentle teasing.

"Oh, here they come now." Trent points at the stage as the Collier's Creek Cowboy Combo enters.

The crowd hoot and cheer as the band members wave at the audience. They've been playing here for as long as I can remember and have a huge following.

"Y'all ready for some good ol' country music?" Georgia asks with a grin, her excitement on par with the rest of the bar.

The band plays—fiddle, banjo, guitar, bass, and drums—and the noise factor and crowd's energy increases as the song goes on.

"Wow, they're great." Kit says. He throws me a grin as he sways to rhythm.

"Right? They're a local favorite," I tell him, my own foot tapping along to the beat. "I thought you'd get a kick out of the full country experience, and it seems like I was right."

He winks. His smile is warm and genuine as we listen to the twang of country tunes and watch the dancing.

A server delivers more food as the band transitions to a ballad, making conversation possible again. We eat—crispy onion rings, golden mozzarella sticks, and steaming hot jalapeño poppers—and talk about everything and nothing. As we joke, Kit's laughter comes freely and his eyes twinkle. He's got small crinkles at the corners when he laughs and his whole face lights up.

When our plates are empty, Georgia stands. "Alright, y'all," she announces. "Let's show this dance floor what we're made of!"

"Sounds like a plan." I'm ready to burn off some of that fried food and haven't been line dancing in ages. I turn to Kit. "Ready to give it a go?"

"Let's do it," he says with a grin, surprising the hell out of me. I expected him to be reluctant, but as we make our way over to join the throng of people already dancing, he looks anything but.

I grab his hand and pull him onto the dance floor. "Come on, let's join in."

"Alright, alright." He laughs as we line up at the back.

"Watch the people in front for the steps, and don't worry if you mess up. The important thing is to have fun!"

"Got it, boss," Kit teases, standing beside me to the left with his hands on his hips. "I'm ready when you are."

I take a deep breath, and give a firm nod, and we're off.

I go left, and Kit goes right. We come to a halt as we bump each other.

"Hey, you're a natural!" I shout over the music.

He smirks. "Must be that great teacher of mine."

We try again, trying to follow the dancers in font. It's a disaster, but a disaster that has us both in stitches. While Georgia and Trent slip directly in line, moving with the other people on the dance floor, Kit and I trip over each other. Kit's laughter is infectious as he bends over and holds his stomach, and I'm grinning from ear to ear.

"See? Isn't this fun?" I ask, my breath coming in short gasps between fits of giggles.

Kit looks at me, his eyes sparkling with happiness, a wide smile across his face. "Yeah, it is."

As the night winds down, Kit and I exchange glances, silently agreeing that it's time for us to go. I can't wait to get home for some alone time. We say our goodbyes to Georgia and Trent and head out into the night.

"Tonight was amazing, Felix," Kit says as we walk to the parking lot. "I never knew line dancing could be so much fun."

I laugh. "I'm not sure you'd call what we did line dancing, but I had a great time."

A slow country ballad starts to play, the melody drifting from the bar.

I stop and grab his hand. "Hey, do you want to dance?"

"Out here?" Kit raises an eyebrow but doesn't seem opposed to the idea.

"Sure, why not? I want to slow dance with you."

In response, he steps closer and places a hand on the small of my back. I wrap my arms around his neck and we begin to sway to the soft music. I'm struck by how easily we fall into step with one another. Nothing like the chaotic shambles of our earlier attempts. We're perfectly in tune as we dance under the chilly night sky.

Kit presses his cheek to mine. "I'm so glad we've gotten to know each other," he murmurs against my ear.

I hum in agreement. "Yeah, me too."

"It means a lot that you've shared so much of your town, of your life, with me. You're a very special man, Felix Montgomery."

My heart leaps at his words, and I tighten my grip on him ever so slightly.

He pulls back to look at me. We're in partial darkness, the light from the Randy's sign too far away for much illumination, but it's bright enough to see Kit's crystal clear blue eyes.

"Hey, can I ask you something?" he says.

"Sure. Anything." I hold my breath, waiting for his question.

His face is serious, his gaze fixed on me. "It's fucking freezing out here. Can we go home?"

I'm not sure what I thought he was going to say but it wasn't that. I burst into laughter. "Kit!"

He grabs my hand and tugs. "I'll slow dance with you all night, so long as we do it naked and in front of the fire."

I don't need any more encouragement and together we run for the car.

CHAPTER NINETEEN

Kit

Placing the wine bottle on the counter, I reach for the corkscrew. I run my thumb over the smooth stainless steel, remembering snatching the opener from Felix the first time he came to dinner at the cabin. We've come a long way since then, although it's only been weeks. Taking the bottle, I peel away the foil to expose the cork, then twist in the corkscrew. The cork comes out with a pop.

Mike wants me back in Seattle next week. He wants to arrange a meeting with my publisher to give them some confidence the new book is back on track. They've been patient up until now, but there's only so much they'll put up with.

I pour the cabernet into two glasses, contemplating leaving all this behind. It feels wrong to walk away from Felix and our relationship, which is just starting to blossom. Sure, we were only supposed to be friends, but what I feel goes well beyond friendship and I know Felix feels it too. Then the doubts resurface. The gossip about the two of us and our age difference. The lingering feeling I'm stopping him from finding someone better, someone more suited to his outgoing, bubbly personality. I'm not sure what he sees in me, but I'm grateful for whatever it is.

"Hey, I'm dying of thirst over here. What are you doing? Helping age the wine?"

His words pull me from my thoughts and I chuckle. He sits cross-legged on the braided rug, shuffling Connect Four chips between his hands. He looks young, and eager, and most of all happy.

I grab the glasses and make my way over, placing them on the coffee table and lowering myself to the floor. My knees crack and Felix raises a brow.

"Don't you say a word!"

"I wouldn't dare," he says. There's laughter in his eyes as he takes his wine.

As we bring our glasses together in a toast, I resolve then and there to make the most of every moment with him, and if that means delaying my return to Seattle, then so be it. I want to give this a chance. I want what we have between us to work more than I want my book to be a success. *Fuck. That's a scary thought.* "Cheers."

The fire crackles, popping and hissing. The cabernet dances on my tongue, and Felix's smile warms my heart. It's a perfect night in.

"So, are you ready?' Felix asks.

"Ready?"

"Ready for me to whip your ass."

I chuckle. "I wouldn't be so cocky. Making rows with round bits of plastic doesn't look too hard. I'll be handing your ass to you on a platter."

"Them's big words, cowboy," Felix says, putting on a country twang. "My cousins and I would play for hours, so I'm pretty much an expert."

"Your cousins?"

Felix nods. "Shawn is my mom's brother, but he doesn't have any kids, so all my cousins are on Dad's side. There are Montgomery's spread all over the county. You might have met one or two. My cousin Mikey works with Georgia at the store, and Sue-Ellen works at the library."

I nod, watching the firelight dance across his face as he tells me stories about his family. My parents are elderly, and not exactly the warm, welcoming type, so I can only imagine the sort of family get-togethers that feature in Felix's life.

"Your family sounds great."

Felix rolls his eyes as he passes me a pile of discs. "I've only been telling you the good stuff. Plus, I've been away, so I'm wearing rose-colored glasses. Do you have a big family?"

I shake my head. "Like you, I'm an only child. Mom had me when she was forty-two, so I was a late in life baby. I grew up with older parents and only one cousin who I haven't seen since I was about ten."

We begin to play, Felix dropping his first disc into the grid. "I like to think the cabins bring families together," he says. "I have so many awesome memories of vacations with my cousins, but also making friends with the kids who were up here with their families for the summer. I'm sorry you missed that."

"And that's why you want to renovate the cabins?" I take a sip of my wine and drop a red disc.

"Sure," he says, dropping a yellow disc, "There's the nostalgia—I want to keep my childhood alive, but I also want other people to experience the same things I did—"

"Like I'm doing now?"

Felix grins. "Exactly. I want to modernize the cabins and attract a whole new generation of people who can enjoy the mountains and the creek."

"And play board games?" I prompt, as I drop another disc.

"Absolutely. There'll always be games." He runs a hand over the old worn-out Connect Four box, then glances at the game of Clue, set aside for the trash because the cards are damaged and pieces missing. Felix's games have had a lot of use.

We play for a while chatting about our favorite board games, before his expression turns serious. He sighs before speaking. "Cam came back sooner than expected."

"Cam?" I'm caught off-guard at the sudden change of topic.

"My friend who owns the coffee shop. He and his husband, Greg, were supposed to be away for six months, but Cam's mom is sick."

"I'm sorry. That's awful. What does that mean for you?" I ask.

There's uncertainty in Felix's eyes. "Well, I was only supposed to manage the coffee shop while he was away on his extended vacation. He says he needs me until the new year, but after that, I'll have to see."

My chest tightens at the idea of Felix leaving to head back to his old life. "Have you thought about what you want to do?" I ask the question but dread the answer.

He shakes his head, brow furrowed. "I'm not sure yet. I guess I could find another job in town or I have contacts in the retail industry back in the city. I mean, that's where my career was before it was derailed so spectacularly, and I should..."

His voice trails off, and I can tell he's weighing bigger decisions, decisions that will probably take him far away. My heart aches—I want to tell him to stay here, to find out what we can have together, but I bite my tongue. He's got the entire world, his entire life, in front of him.

"This is your chance to choose exactly what you want," I say, trying my best to sound upbeat. "Exciting times ahead, right?"

Felix gives me a small smile. I reach out and squeeze his hand, hoping he understands how much I care. How much I want his happiness.

Felix takes a deep breath. "I'm scared of making the wrong choice. What would you do?"

Fuck! I'd stay in Collier's Creek and make a life with you.

I clear my throat. "I can't tell you what to do. You need to do whatever feels right, Felix. Life's about taking chances and making mistakes. The good thing is that your family and friends will always be here for you, no matter what path you take." I pause for a moment. "I'll be here for you."

"You will?" His voice wavers with uncertainty.

I force a smile and squeeze his hand again. "Of course. Whatever you decide."

He looks at me for a long moment. "Thank you."

CHAPTER TWENTY

Felix

I'm running late but can't summon even the slightest bit of regret. Those extra few minutes with Kit were worth every bit of the hassling I'm bound to get from my friends. For a second I'm disappointed he's not with me, but the twinkling lights and festive garlands adorning the lampposts lift my mood. Collier's Creek looks like a holiday card.

Stepping out into the brisk night air, I'm grateful I got a park not too far from the restaurant. My breath clouds before me as I step carefully onto the sidewalk. I love the snow and cold that come with Christmas—the holiday season in Florida with Mom and Dad just isn't the same.

Fox's Restaurant is ablaze with lights, and warmth greets me as I step inside. Shrugging my coat, I look around and spot Cam, Greg, and Georgia seated in one of the beige booths at the back.

"Well, look who finally made it!" Cam says as I slip in beside Georgia. His grin is wide, eyes crinkling at the corners. It's good to see him smiling and I hope that means his mom is doing better.

Georgia arches one eyebrow. "We were about to send out a search party."

"Yeah, thanks for finally joining us," Greg jokes.

I hold up both hands in mock surrender. "Sorry, I got caught up helping with something in the cabins."

"Uh huh, likely story," Georgia says with a smirk. "I bet we can guess what you were helping with."

She makes air quotes around "helping" and I'm sure I blush because she's not far off the mark.

"What are you drinking?" Greg asks.

"I'm driving, so I'll stick to Coke, thanks."

Greg motions to Fiona, who comes over to serve us. We make small talk until she returns with my drink and then takes our food orders.

"So, Cam, how's your mom doing?" I ask.

His expression turns serious. "The treatment is going okay so far. There are signs of remission and she's still got a long road in front of her, but she's being positive. To be honest, I'm not sure how she does it."

Georgia reaches over and squeezes his hand. "We're here for you guys, whatever you need."

Cam smiles. "Thanks. I don't know what I'd do without you all."

"Luckily, you never have to find out," she replies. "I'll always be here for you."

Her words remind me I need to finalize my decision, because leaving Collier's Creek is still on the table. But, even if Cam doesn't need me to manage the coffee shop after next month, he still needs my support.

Cam takes a deep breath. "Anyway, enough about all that. We're here to celebrate Christmas. We've got something we want to show you. Greg, have you got the photos?"

Greg pulls out his phone, brings up some pictures, and passes it across. The photos are of a house. It's not very large but has a pretty garden out the front. It looks familiar.

"Is that the cottage down past the school?" I ask.

Greg nods. "It is, and it's all ours."

"Oh! You bought a house!" Georgia's voice is loud in the restaurant and a few heads turn.

"Shh." I nudge her and chuckle before looking at Cam. He is grinning from ear-to-ear. "Congrats, man. That's fantastic. I'm so happy for you guys."

"It needs a lot of work," Cam says.

Greg leans in to his side. "But we're up to the job, right, babe?"

They look at each other, and the love between them is obvious.

"Aww. Next you'll be telling us you're having kids," Georgia teases.

Cam and Greg exchange a look, then Cam throws another of those grins.

"OMG you really are!" Georgia says.

Cam nods. "We're talking about starting a family soon."

Georgia's bouncing in her seat. "I can't wait for a little Greg or Cam Junior to be running around."

"They could have a girl," I say, then smile at the guys. "But a kid? That would be amazing."

"Hold your horses," Greg says. "One step at a time. We're only talking about it at this stage. There's a lot to consider and even if we were ready, it's a fucking complicated process."

"You'll be great dads when the time's right," I say. I've known Cam since I was a kid, and I've known Greg for ages. I watched them fall in love, I've seen them deal with Greg's accident, and lately seen how strong they are together as they deal with Cam's family's problems. I have no doubt they'll nail the parenthood thing.

"Anyway," Greg says. "Enough about us. What about you, Georgia? Any romance on the horizon?"

Her cheeks flush pink. "Maybe. I've gone on a few dates with Trent from the bank. He's really sweet."

Cam leans in. "Okay, time to give us all the deets!"

As Georgia gushes about Trent, I think about my own future here in Collier's Creek. My friends' dreams remind me how precious life and friendship is. It feels right being here surrounded by the people I care about most. I take a sip of my beer. Kit was right—a night out with them was exactly what I needed.

Fiona brings over our meals and conversation stops for a moment as we all get stuck into the delicious food. I look across at the open kitchen where I see Fiona's wife, Mai, the restaurant owner. I raise my hand and she waves in return.

"Felix. You haven't told us how things are going with Kit," Cam eventually says. "He seems like a good guy the couple of times I've met him."

I smile, like I always seem to do when thinking about Kit. "He is. I've really enjoyed getting to know him these past months."

"He's certainly come out of his shell since he met you," Georgia adds. "When he first arrived in town, Kit hardly said boo to anyone. He holed up in the cabin with his writing, right, Felix?"

I put down my knife and fork. "He's been working to a deadline, but he's let me drag him out a time or two. We went to Sweetwater Falls and since then we've been exploring the area when the weather allows."

"And what do you do on the days when it's too cold and blustery outside?" Georgia asks. There's a glint in her eye that I know only too well.

"Board games, Georgia, we play board games," I reply, trying to keep a straight face. "Can't say I recommend playing Scrabble against an author, though, or any word game, actually."

She places her hand on mine where it rests on the table. "You really like him, don't you?"

"I really do." My chest fills with warmth just thinking about him—how he lights up when we're trying new things, his willingness to give line dancing a go, the way he looks at me when we're debating any topic, listening to my every word. He makes me feel special. Cherished.

"I'm so glad you've found happiness again," Cam says. "Now I don't feel so bad dragging you back to our little neck of the woods."

Greg laughs. "Next you'll be claiming matchmaker rights."

"Well, if I didn't ask Felix to manage CC's then he'd never run into Kit when he bought his morning coffee, then—"

"Umm, guys. Kit's staying at the cabins. Don't you think Felix would have run into him there?"

Cam huffs and waves a hand. "Semantics. Anyway, all the matters is that Felix has found love."

I grin at that. I might not have said the words, but love is absolutely what I feel in my heart. Big fucking love. I swallow heavily, emotions threatening to overwhelm. I feel so damn much that it's going to nearly kill me if it's taken away.

"Felix. What's wrong?"

I look across and see concern on my friends' faces. Georgia squeezes my hand again. "Are you okay?"

"Yes. No. Fuck, I don't know." I take a deep breath. "I'm second-guessing myself."

"About Kit?"

"No. Not about Kit. He's amazing," I'm quick to reassure. There's not a doubt in my mind about how I feel about him. "Maybe that's part of the problem."

"Huh?" Cam furrows his brow.

"Now you're back and you'll be taking over the coffee shop again soon, I need to figure out what's next for me."

"And Kit's getting in the way?" Georgia asks.

"Not exactly, but my feelings are. I love being back and I want to stay in Collier's Creek. but what if I'm making the decision for all the wrong reasons? What if I'm letting my feelings for Kit override everything else?"

"Making a decision for love is as good a reason as any, if you ask me," Cam says. Greg nods and smiles softly at him. Those two have seen each other through thick and thin.

"You said you love being back in town and hanging with us, and I know you've enjoyed your time at CC's," Georgia says. "Plus, I've never heard you happier than when you've been sharing your plans for the cabins. Oh, except when you've been going on and on about Kit." She laughs, then continues. "So I don't think it's just Kit drawing you back here, hon."

What she says makes sense. Kit being here plays a massive role in my desire to stay in Collier's Creek, but it's not the only thing.

"Maybe you need to ask yourself if you'd make Collier's Creek your home again, even if Kit wasn't here," Greg suggests.

"Collier's Creek will always be my home." There's no question about that. "You don't think I gave up too easily, running home when things got tough, though?" I ask. I've been thinking a lot about my old job lately. It feels like I left things unfinished. Getting a degree… for what?

"Maybe all that went down was a positive thing—gave you the shove you needed," Cam says.

"Let me ask you this?" Georgia says. "If Kit left tomorrow, would you want to rush back to your old life? Find a new apartment in the city? Get a new job and return to the corporate life?"

I picture myself in a tiny one-bedroom apartment, back to commuting to the office, and dealing with office politics. The thought makes me shudder. "That'd be a no."

"I thought so."

"The idea of working with Uncle Shawn to build the cabin business is exciting. I hate to think about leaving and not being part of it."

"It sounds like you have your answer," Georgia says. "I've never seen you happier."

"It's just hard not to second-guess myself sometimes." I take another swig of Coke. "This adulting stuff is the pits."

Cam laughs and shakes his finger. "Listen to me. You deserve to be happy. Truly happy. Whatever that looks like."

"He's right," Georgia says. "Don't let fear hold you back from the life you want. Seize the moment, remember?"

I let their words sink in. They're saying the exact same thing Kit said to me just a week ago.

CHAPTER TWENTY-ONE

Kit

The lights of the small Christmas tree in the corner cast a warm glow on the walls and give the cabin an even cozier feel than usual. The fire crackles in the hearth as soft Christmas music plays from the Bluetooth speaker on the mantle. For the first time in years, I've allowed myself to be surrounded by the spirit of Christmas. The warmth of the fire, the smell of pine, and the festive decorations remind me of happier times, times that feel are within my grasp again. I spent last Christmas with Mom and Dad at a hotel buffet in Seattle. But this year, with Felix and his family, feels like the first proper Christmas in a long time.

It's thanks to Felix that I have a tree. He dragged me out to cut the small sapling and provided a boxful of decorations, half of which I'm sure he made when he was a kid. I sit on the floor beside the tree and can't help smiling at the little Christmas tree hanging from one of the branches. The tiny Christmas tree is made from a stick with green ribbons tied at various intervals and a red button glued to the top to look like a miniature tree.

I tear my gaze away from the tree and focus on the box in front of me, carefully folding the wrapping paper around Felix's gift, ensuring that each corner is neat. I secure the paper in place with tape before moving on to tie a neat bow with a red ribbon. I haven't put this much effort into wrapping a gift in years, but for Felix, I want to. I hold the finished gift up and admire my handiwork for a moment. It's only a simple present and I hope he likes it.

My stomach is in knots, nerves refusing to settle—a strange nervous excitement for the day ahead. I want to enjoy the celebration, but I hate the idea it could be the only holiday I share with Felix. I place the gift beneath the tree, then look up at the sound of boots on the porch. *Just in time.*

Felix bursts into the cabin, letting in a draft of cold air. He quickly shuts the door, shrugs off his coat, and unwinds the scarf from his neck then turns, face lighting when he sees me at the tree. "Hey."

"Hey, you." I grin up at him.

He crosses the room, dropping a kiss to my lips as he kneels beside me on the rug.

"Is that all the greeting I get?" I say, pulling him to me.

His face is cold against mine, and he laughs as he falls into my lap. I press my mouth to his, conveying all the emotion I feel into the kiss. His lips are cool, but his tongue is warm as it darts out to meet mine, deepening the kiss. When we finally part, Felix is flushed, his lips swollen, his eyes dark.

"That's better." I smirk.

"I could get used to coming home to a welcome like that," Felix says.

So could I.

I can't think of anything better than knowing Felix was coming home to me each day, but my chest tightens at the knowledge this may be a fantasy. I push the thought aside, focusing on the here and now. I want this to be a special Christmas, a new special memory I can tuck away for the future.

"What took you so long? I thought you'd be back a while ago."

"Mom had a list a mile long of things she needed me to do, so it took longer than expected. I see you've been busy here." He smiles and gestures to the gift I've just placed under the tree.

"I know we're supposed to spend Christmas with your family, but I wanted to give you your gift now, while it's just the two of us."

Felix grins from ear to ear. "I *love* that idea."

"Don't get too excited," I warn. "It's nothing big."

"I'm sure I'll love it no matter what it is," Felix says, then destroys the sentimental moment. "And if I don't, there's always Facebook MarketPlace or re-gifting."

I burst into laughter and lift him from my lap so I can reach the gift. "Well, here goes nothing."

Felix sits beside me and takes the box, brushing his fingers along the ribbon as if it's the most precious thing he's ever held in his hands. When he looks up and meets my gaze, his eyes are shining. I wish I could give him the world.

"Thank you," he murmurs and I'm suddenly nervous. *What if he thinks it's stupid?*

Instead of ripping off the paper like I expected, Felix takes his time. He undoes the bow, then takes off the ribbon before gently peeling off the tape. Only then does he pull back the paper to reveal the box within.

His eyes light up as he sees the board game. He runs a finger over the game title. I hope he's remembering all the evenings we've spent playing games by the fire.

"This is awesome." He reaches over and wraps his arms around me in a tight hug, the game squashed between us. When he pulls away, he lifts the box again. "Can we play tonight?"

"Sure." I grin. "But I can already tell you it's Professor Plum with the candlestick in the library."

"Oh! It is, is it?" Felix's laughter fills the room. He tilts his head and narrows his eyes. "I guess you are the master of mysteries."

"Hardly." I chuckle. "It took me forever to get that damn book finished."

"All the same, maybe we'll stick to Monopoly." There's amusement in his eyes, then his face softens. "But seriously, thank you. It's the perfect gift."

"You're welcome."

"I have something for you too. It's not as fancy, but I hope you'll like it."

Felix retrieves a thin rectangular package from behind the Christmas tree and passes it over. The wrapping is simple, a natural brown paper tied with twine. There's a white gift tag tucked under the twine. It's tiny, with only room for "To Kit from Felix" but he's scrawled a tiny heart next to his name that makes me tingly inside.

"Thank you." I unwrap the gift, discretely pocketing the little card. I'll treasure the small memento of our time together.

The present is a surprise. I raise my eyes to meet his gaze. "You had this made for me?"

He nods, a small smile lifting his lip. "For when you're working at your desk."

The mouse mat displays a stylized map of Collier's Creek. I run my finger over the familiar streets and landmarks—CC's, of course, Sweetwater Falls, the bookstore, Randy's, and other places we've visited together.

I lift my head again to find him studying me. "It's amazing. To make sure I never forget my time here?"

"Something like that," Felix says, his brown eyes twinkling. "I wanted to give you something that would remind you of Collier's Creek—and maybe tempt you to come back."

"Trust me," I say, my voice wobbling as I look at the gift in my hands. "There's no way I'm going to forget this place. Or you."

Felix reaches out to intertwine his fingers with mine. "I'm glad," he whispers, then presses a tender kiss to my cheek.

My eyes prickle, so I look at the mouse mat again. The detail is amazing. It's then I notice the cute sign drawn at the location of the cabins. "Felix lives here."

"Wait," I say, suddenly realizing the implications and pointing at the tiny detail. "Does this mean you're staying in Collier's Creek?"

He nods. "I've decided this is where I want to stay. I want to work with Uncle Shawn and expand the business. There's so much potential and I want to be part of it. Besides, Uncle Shawn can't do it by himself. My friends are here... there are so many reasons."

I know how much this decision was weighing on him so I'm happy for him. If only I felt the same about returning to my own life. "I'm so proud of you. I know making the decision about your future wasn't easy, but I'm happy you've found something you're passionate about."

"I'm happy too," he says, but a little light is gone from his eyes.

However, before I can question him, Felix is on his feet and hauling me to mine. "Come on. Mom will have our guts for garters if we're late for lunch."

FELIX'S PARENTS WELCOME ME with open arms, and I'm touched by their easy acceptance of me in their lives. I immediately feel part of the family as Susan puts me to work in the kitchen while Felix, his dad, Brian, and Uncle Shawn head out to drop off some last-minute gifts to some friends in the area.

Felix plants a quick kiss to my cheek as he leaves me in the kitchen. "Good luck."

He chuckles as his mom pushes him from the room. "Get away with you."

Susan passes me the potato masher and maneuvers me in front of a large pot of drained potatoes. "Here you go. Give these a good going over."

"I'm not much of a cook."

She chuckles and I see where Felix gets his smile from. "Mashing isn't cooking, dear. You can't really go wrong. So, tell me a little about yourself."

Good lord. I plunge the masher into the pot. "I... umm. I'm an author, but I'm not very interesting I'm afraid."

"Everyone is interesting." She drops a knob of butter into the potato. "Do you have any family, Kit?"

I can hear the unasked question. Why are you here with us instead of spending the holidays with your family? "Just my parents."

"And you're not close, I assume?" Susan says, as she opens the oven and checks on a huge turkey. The scent is heavenly. The door closes with a bang.

"I don't think my mom and dad are cut out to be parents."

Susan places a hand on my forearm. "I'm sorry to hear that, but you have us now. Brian and I may live in another state, but we're still part of Felix's life and the Collier's Creek community. Now, how's that mashed potato coming along?"

I'm pleased she doesn't try to tell me it isn't too late, that I can try to build some kind of relationship with my parents beyond an occasional phone call. I offer her a smile and tilt the pot her way so she can see inside. "How about a little butter and some salt?" I suggest.

She winks. "And who said you can't cook?"

"Felix has been giving me lessons," I say as she adds a knob of butter and a generous sprinkling of salt. "He said you taught him the family recipes, and he's been sharing them with me."

"He's been giving away the family's secret recipes!" She feigns indignation, but her face dissolves into a smile.

"You've raised an amazing man, Susan. I don't know what I would have done without him." I keep focusing on the mash as I talk. "I don't know if Felix has told you much, but I've been in a dark place since losing my partner. Felix refused to let me wallow in that cabin. He made me see all the things I was missing by shutting myself away." *Missing laughter, and friendship, and love.*

"From what I've heard, you've done a lot for him too."

I raise a brow.

"Felix has faced his own challenges," Susan says. "We wanted him to find his own way in life, not feel as if he didn't have any choices. We encouraged him to leave the nest, and I always wondered if we'd done the right thing. You see, it wasn't really Felix's choice to move away, it was ours."

"You only wanted what was best for him," I say.

She nods. "He's our only child..."

My chest tightens at her words. I'm an only child too, but my mother is nothing like Susan, who only has her son's best interests at heart. "He's lucky to have you."

She gives a small smile. "It's hard to let go of the ones you love. Selfishly, you just want to wrap them in cotton wool and keep them safe, but there's a whole wide world out there."

"That's true, but there's so much here too, Susan. Collier's Creek will always be home to Felix."

"Yes, I can see that he belongs here. Thank you for supporting him in his decision."

"I didn't do anything. He made up his own mind."

"You allowed him to make his own choices and for that, I'm grateful." She pauses and lowers her eyes for a moment before raising them to meet mine. "To be honest, I was worried you'd influence him, encourage him to follow you to... to wherever you're going next. You've seen more of the world."

"I agree. I'm at a different stage in my life. I'm older but—"

She grabs hold of my arm. "Your age has nothing to do with it, Kit. The age difference doesn't matter to me. I can see how much you mean to Felix, and I was worried Felix would put you first before himself."

"Felix is a strong man. He puts other people first, but he knows what he wants."

Susan nods. "And you helped give him the confidence to grab his future with both hands."

"There's no doubt in my mind that Felix can achieve whatever he puts his mind to, and if that's choosing the cabins and the community here, then I'm happy for him." Inwardly I know that's not quite true—while I'm happy for Felix, I'm only truly happy if I'm here by his side.

"I can see why my son is so enamored." Susan's face softens, her brown eyes that are so similar to Felix's crinkling at the corners. "Do you love my boy?"

"Yes," I respond instantly.

"Then that's all I need to know."

She pulls me into a hug before straightening. She sniffs, her eyes glistening, as she adjusts her apron. "Now, the turkey's ready. Can you give me a hand to get it out of the oven?"

CHRISTMAS DINNER IS FESTIVE and relaxed. There are just the five of us, but enough food to ensure there will be leftovers for days. The conversation flows easily and I'm enthralled watching Felix throughout the meal. His eyes shine with happiness, and the smile doesn't leave his face.

Susan and Brian are sitting next to each other. They share fleeting touches and jokes, gently teasing each other in a way that makes it clear how much love there is between them. It's something I want. Every now and then, Susan meets my gaze with a knowing look, as if she can read my thoughts.

Uncle Shawn isn't left out. I can see the family making every effort to keep his spirits up, and he's surprisingly resilient. He shares a story about his late wife, Maureen, and the moment is bittersweet.

When the conversation turns to the cabin development, the mood changes, brightening again. Everyone is excited by the prospect of revamping the business and hang on every word Felix says. When Uncle Shawn asks Felix some questions, my chest swells with pride. I know how much research he's done and how much time he's spent on business plans, and it's great to see his expertise recognized.

"What do you think, Kit?" Brian asks, turning to me. "You've had firsthand experience staying in the cabins."

"The ideas for the upgrades are perfect. A little more modern and comfortable but still in keeping with the rustic location," I say, but to be honest, my stay has been perfect, faulty electrics and all. I wouldn't change any of it.

Felix leans closer, his voice low and filled with warmth. "I'm so glad you're here, Kit. Having your input means a lot to us."

My chest warms and I smile. I'm glad I'm here too.

"Of course, we'll have to temporarily close the cabins for a couple of months during renovations," Brian says.

"I guess that means you're evicting me then," I joke.

The others laugh, but when my gaze turns to Felix, he's drained of color, mouth drawn in a tight line.

"It's time I find somewhere else to live anyway," I say, placing a hand on his thigh. "I need a proper study and more space for all my stuff."

Felix's eyes widen, and I wonder if he's realizing that I'm planning on sticking around. "Your stuff?"

"Sure. I can only live out of a suitcase for so long. It's time I found somewhere more permanent."

It's as if time slows down for just a moment as he registers the weight of my words. His gaze locking onto mine with an intensity that makes my heart race.

"Wait, you mean... you're staying?" he asks, voice thick with emotion.

"Of course I'm staying," I reply softly. There was no question, really. Not after I've given my heart to him. I try to convey all that in a look. I wish I could say more—there's so much more I want to say—but it's not the place, not with his family looking on.

Our emotional moment is interrupted by Uncle Shawn. "I'll introduce you to Geraldine's niece. She owns the local real estate."

As the conversation around us resumes, I look at each person in the room—Uncle Shawn, Susan, and Brian, who already feel like family, and then Felix—and I know I've made the right decision. This is where I belong.

A while later, after coffee and Christmas fudge, we make our farewells. Susan kisses my cheek, and Brian pulls me in for a fierce hug, clapping me on the back.

"I'll drop your gifts around tomorrow," Uncle Shawn says as we're putting on our coats, indicating the small pile near the tree.

Susan presses a container of leftovers into Felix's hands. "Now get going, quickly, before your dad tries to rope Kit into staying for another drink."

Felix chuckles. "Thanks, Mom." He turns to me. "Come on, let's go home."

Home.

My spirits are high, my heart warm as we step outside into the crisp, snowy night, our breath visible in the cold air. The moon casts a silvery glow on the snow-covered ground, lighting our way as our boots crunch in the snow. As we walk hand in hand toward my cabin, I feel as if we're walking through a magical wonderland.

Felix leads me along the winding path until we arrive at the cabin. The lights on the small Christmas tree are twinkling, carols still playing softly, and the lamps bathe the room in a soft glow. It doesn't take long to stoke the fire back to life. We sit on the rug in front of the flames, my back against the couch,

Felix between my legs, his back pressed to my front, my arms wrapped around his waist. It's been a long day, and it's perfect to end it with just the two of us.

"Kit," Felix says softly, breaking the silence between us, "do you ever think about... you know, what's next for us?"

"Of course." I give him a reassuring squeeze. "I think about it all the time."

"And that's why you're staying in Collier's Creek?" His voice trembles slightly.

I realize he needs to hear the words, and giving my heart to someone else isn't something that scares me anymore so the words will come easy. "Hey, look at me."

He scoots around until we're face to face.

"I'm staying in Collier's Creek because that's where you are. I can't think of anywhere I'd rather be."

His smile lights up the room. "It means so much that you're staying here. With me. Thank you."

"It's me who should thank you, Felix, You've given me more than you could ever know. I love you."

"I love you too," he whispers, his eyes swimming with emotion.

He pulls me into a tight embrace. As I relax into his hold, inhaling his scent, feeling his heart beating against mine, I'm filled with a sense of hope and excitement for the future. I'm looking forward to whatever comes our way.

Epilogue

Eight months later

Kit

The sun filters through the canopy above as Felix and I hike up the winding trail to Sweetwater Falls. My muscles burn, but the sight of Felix in front of me—the sunlight reflecting off his blond hair, his shoulders stretching the fabric of his T-shirt—spurs me on.

We've had a busy few months, and I'm glad Felix is taking the day off. He works hard and deserves some time for himself. The cabin renovation is complete, but Felix is already on to stage two of the development. Plans are underway for glamping tents that will showcase the absolute beauty of the property in the foothills of the mountains and be perfect in the summer months. I couldn't be prouder of what he's achieved.

We round the corner and there they are—Sweetwater Falls—the first place I opened my heart to Felix.

He turns to me, eyes shining. "Isn't it beautiful?"

I nod, though I'm not looking at the falls. "Gorgeous."

"I've been here so many times, but they still take my breath away," he says.

"Mine too." I step up to him. "Every fucking time."

We've been together nearly a year now—eight months since we admitted our feelings properly for the first time—and my feelings have only grown stronger with each passing day.

I wrap an arm around him and draw him close. "I love you."

He rises up on his toes, looping his arms around my neck. "I love you too."

We kiss in the sunshine and I want to capture this moment forever—it's perfect.

I reluctantly let him go. "Come on, let's get the picnic set up."

We spread out our blanket and unpack cheese, crusty bread, strawberries, and a bottle of white wine. Felix pours us each some into plastic tumblers.

I raise my glass to toast. "Here's to Sweetwater Lodge."

"Sweetwater Lodge." He touches his glass to mine.

"Seriously, Felix. I'm so proud of what you've achieved. You came up with the idea and you've worked your ass off to see your vision come to life."

Felix ducks his head, a flush rising on his cheeks. I love that I still have the power to make him blush.

"You helped with the renaming by suggesting Sweetwater Lodge."

"Only because you shared your special place with me."

"We make a good team," he says.

"That we do."

The wine is delicious and so is our picnic spread. There's something about the mountain air that makes even the simplest of foods taste special. We nibble on cheese while we sip the wine, passing morsels to each other. Eventually, we lie back and stare at the wide blue sky.

"I saw your publisher called again," Felix eventually says. "They really want you to do that book tour."

I turn my head to look at him. He has his hands under his head, looking up at the sky, not at me.

"Yeah, they're persistent. They want to cement my status as the king of cozy mystery, and publicity and a tour will maximize sales. I've already told Mike I won't do it."

Felix rolls to his side to face me, propping his head on a hand. "I don't want to hold you back. This is your big chance to make a comeback after being out of the industry for so long."

"You're not holding me back from anything. I'm happy here."

"You don't want to stay in expensive hotels while seeing the world as your adoring fans fall at your feet?"

It suddenly occurs to me that maybe I'm the one holding Felix back. Maybe he'd like to experience that kind of life. I don't think so, but I throw it out there, anyway. "I'd do it if you wanted to. If you wanted to come with me."

"God no!"

He sits up and I echo his movements until we're facing each other cross-legged on the blanket.

"You honestly don't want to live it up?" I ask.

"Cross my heart. I'd like to travel someday, maybe see some of those places you've mentioned or explore somewhere new, but criss-crossing the country isn't for me."

Relief floods through me. "I don't want that kind of life either. I'm happy here with you and our friends, and you know I prefer writing romance these days."

Felix smiles, eyes crinkling. "Lots of inspiration."

"Absolutely." I grin as I reach out and take his hand. "You know, I had an idea. I can't ignore my publisher and readers completely, and Mike will just keep hassling, so I was thinking of a compromise."

He tilts his head and his brow furrows. "What did you have in mind?"

"A book release party at Ellis Books. No cameras or interviews, just a chance to celebrate with the community. I mean, they've all shown so much support, you know? I can organize catering, I'll read an excerpt from the new book, and sign copies for anyone who wants one."

"I think your students would love that."

I've been teaching some creative writing classes at the library for the last six weeks. It wasn't something I planned on doing, but it turns out I love discussing the craft of writing and sharing my knowledge and experience.

"It's a brilliant idea, Kit," Felix continues. "It's a great way to give back to your readers here without the fuss of a big tour. Gramps will be honored you want to host it at his store. I'm sure he's still a little star-struck that a famous author regularly visits his little bookshop."

I huff a laugh. "I'm hardly famous. My books may be well known, but I'm just a small town writer leading a simple life and I aim to keep it that way."

"So no regrets, leaving that all behind?" Felix asks.

"Not a single one."

"Thank God for that." Felix grins, that dimple of his flashing, and gets to his knees, nearly knocking over the wine bottle in the process. "Oops."

He laughs as I lunge for the bottle. I set it up against the rock and by the time I turn back, Felix is holding a small dark blue velvet box. My breath catches in my throat. "Felix."

He opens the box to reveal two platinum bands nestled inside. "Marry me."

I look at him in awe. I can't believe how lucky I am to have this man in my life. As I see the love reflected back at me, there's not a doubt in my mind.

"Yes."

That one word is all that's needed to seal my future with Felix.

He surges forward and throws his arms around my neck, claiming me in a passionate kiss. The kiss is over way too soon, but I can't complain because he takes my hand and slips a ring on my finger.

"There. You can't change your mind."

My eyes prickle as I chuckle. It's so like Felix to bring some lightness to the solemn moment.

I blink against the tears as I take the other ring and place it on his finger.

Sunshine glints off the band, the symbol of our commitment to each other. I take his hand in mine and pull him to me. "I love you," I murmur against his lips. This time, the kiss is gentle and my heart overflows with happiness at finding my happy ending with Felix in my arms.

It's the best happily ever after I could wish for.

COLLIER'S CREEK SERIES

Thank you for reading *Blue Skies*. I hope you enjoyed the story and spending time with Kit and Felix.

Blue Skies is the last book in the Collier's Creek series that starts with **Best Kind of Awkward** by Becca Seymour. So if you enjoyed meeting Will and haven't read book one yet, make sure you check out book one to see Will and Colton get their happily ever after.

Best Kind of Awkward by Becca Seymour

Mandatory Repairs by Elle Keaton

Sheriff of the Creek by Sue Brown

All the Wrong Pages by Katherine McIntyre

Meeting Mr Adorkable by Ali Ryecart

Blue Skies by Nic Starr

About The Author

NIC STARR

Nic Starr lives in Australia where she tries to squeeze as much into her busy life as possible. Balancing the demands of a corporate career with raising a family and writing can be challenging, but she wouldn't give it up for the world. Always a reader, the lure of m/ m romance was strong and she devoured hundreds of wonderful m/ m romance books before eventually realising she had some stories of her own that needed to be told! When not writing or reading, she loves to spend time with her family— an understanding husband and two beautiful daughters— and is often found indulging in her love of cooking and planning her dream home in the country.

Scan the QR code or visit Nic's website to find out more about her social media and newsletter.

Website: www.nicstarr.com

READ MORE GAY ROMANCE FROM NIC STARR

Wild Card

Hitting the big time in Australia isn't enough. Making it overseas, now that's on a whole other level.

Rafe Moreno, lead singer of HyperOctane, is on the brink of achieving everything he's set out to do before his thirtieth birthday. Ten years of hard work and focus is finally paying off. Not that he doesn't enjoy the rock and roll lifestyle—adoration, parties, men. What's not to like? Including a hot hook-up with his bandmate's younger brother. But the most important thing is keeping his eye on the prize at any cost. Parker Shaw is nothing like his outgoing, super-talented rock star brother, so finding himself on a plane heading to the other side of the world to play guitar with HyperOctane is insane.

Who in their right mind would want an ordinary, skinny, red-haired analyst to perform with one of the top bands from Australia?

Rafe's dream is the big time, not a relationship. The furthest thing from Parker's mind is trusting his broken heart to anyone again. But what happens on the road, stays on the road, right? Rafe and Parker embark on the rock tour of a lifetime, a tour that will bring a lot more than they expected, because love is a wild card, not something you can plan for.

Wild Card is an opposites attract, forced proximity, rock star romance.

Buy at: books2read.com/wild-card

Rustic Melody

Can a boy from the country and a guy from the city ever make it work?

Adam Chambers has never seen eye-to-eye with his father and is reluctant to take over the family's property-development company. To clear his head and work out what he wants to do with the rest of his life, Adam leaves his responsibilities in the city and heads out to see the country.
He isn't much closer to deciding what to do with his life when he arrives at one of Australia's largest events, the Tamworth Country Music Festival, and meets Joey Callaway.
Since Joey's father's tragic death left Joey the family's debt-ridden pub, Joey has struggled, desperate to turn the business around and give his mum the life she deserves. A break away from the pressures of running the pub is just what he needs, and a hook-up with Adam is the perfect way to forget about his troubles.
The one-night stand might just be an opening act. If Adam and Joey can follow the music in their hearts, perhaps they can heal each other and create a melody that will last a lifetime.

Rustic Melody is an Australian small town romance story.

Buy at: books2read.com/rusticmelody

Charlie's Hero

Rejection may try to tear them apart, but will ultimately bring them together.

Schoolteacher Charlie Matthews returns to his hometown seeking the life he's been missing since coming out. He wants simple things——friendship and a sense of belonging——and it looks like his dreams are coming true when an accident brings Josh into his life.

When paramedic Josh Campbell attends an emergency and meets Charlie, sparks fly. He's found the one person who makes him feel whole and who he wants to build a future with. But the thought of being rejected by his brother, the man who sacrificed everything for him, is overwhelming.

For Charlie to have his happy ever after, he needs Josh to take a chance, but is their love strong enough motivation for Josh? And if Josh's worst fears come true, can their relationship survive the fallout?

It's not until Charlie confronts his own past that he fully understands what Josh has to lose. But Josh is Charlie's hero, and Josh will do anything to prove to Charlie that his dreams can come true.

Charlie's Hero is low angst m/m romance set in a small town, featuring first responders and found families.

Buy at: books2read.com/charlieshero

Printed in Great Britain
by Amazon